ABOUT THIS BOOK

Welcome to Havenwood Falls, a small town in the majestic mountains of Colorado. A town where legacies began centuries ago, bloodlines run deep, and dark secrets abound. A town where nobody is what you think, where truths pose as lies, and where myths blend with reality. A place where everyone has a story. Including the high schoolers. This is only but one . . .

This sequel to *Bound by Shadows* continues the story of Eris and Rylan.

Rylan Gilles has found a new life in Havenwood Falls. A better one. One with a new pack, a new family, friends, a job, and even a girlfriend. He vows to himself to never allow his past to interfere with his future. But when an enemy of his father, a psychotic shifter named Lars, hunts down and kills his old pack's alpha, they turn to Rylan to lead and save them.

Eris Blaekthorn has been working on growing her newfound magical powers, and with that has come intense nightmares that feel more like premonitions. Horrifying images of a large dark shifter ripping Rylan to shreds and killing him plague her dreams. But when she tries to discuss these with Rylan, he shuts her out.

Dead set on keeping his personal vow, Rylan's determined to handle Lars on his own, but Eris knows where this will end. She hopes he'll turn to her and his new pack for help, while she fears that he'll do the opposite. If he faces Lars alone, her nightmares may soon turn to reality. But if he doesn't, he risks losing everything, including the girl he loves.

SHADOWS & SPELLS

A HAVENWOOD FALLS HIGH NOVELLA

CAMEO RENAE

HAVENWOOD FALLS HIGH BOOKS

Written in the Stars by Kallie Ross

Reawakened by Morgan Wylie

The Fall by Kristen Yard

Somewhere Within by Amy Hale

Awaken the Soul by Michele G. Miller

Bound by Shadows by Cameo Renae

Inamorata by Randi Cooley Wilson

Fata Morgana by E.J. Fechenda

Forever Emeline by Katie M. John

Reclamation by AnnaLisa Grant

Avenoir by Daniele Lanzarotta

Avenge the Heart by Michele G. Miller

Curse the Night by R.K. Ryals

Blood & Iron by Amy Hale

Shadows & Spells by Cameo Renae

Falling Deep by J.L. Weil

Saving Infiniti by Rose Garcia (December 2018)

Willful by Liz Ferry (January 2019)

More books releasing on a monthly basis.

Stay up to date at www.HavenwoodFalls.com

To all the Havenwood Falls Authors.
Because of you, my characters have the coolest places to hang out, and the most awesome peeps to interact with. Thank you! You all rock!

CHAPTER 1

ERIS

*I*t was after midnight when Rylan pulled his motorcycle into the vacant parking lot of a small motel. There was one flickering streetlamp, which added to the already eerie vibe in the air.

But just down the road, an illuminated grocery mart sign gave away his location. He was in Montrose.

I sensed something dark, menacing, and evil nearby. My eyes scoured the area, desperately searching for something I could feel but couldn't see. Then, I saw them—a pair of blood-red eyes, lurking in the shadows. Watching Rylan. Stalking him.

Rylan slid off his bike, his attention on a small piece of paper—the one the girl Keira had given him a few weeks ago at the Festival of Lights. It was the location of the rest of the pack.

With Rylan's attention averted, I heard a faint guttural growl that made the hair on my body stand on end. The wolf was downwind, which was why Rylan couldn't smell him. Sneaky bastard.

The beast was large and crouched in an attack position. I could see the want in his wicked eyes, hear it in his terrible growl.

"Rylan!" I screamed, as the wolf bounded toward him.

Before Rylan could figure out what was going on and shift, the huge wolf pounced.

Sharp teeth sunk into Rylan's neck. Then, a sickening crack shattered the air.

"No!" I wailed, running toward him.

Rylan lay on the ground. His throat was gone, torn flesh hanging in its place, while blood pooled around him. His eyes—those beautiful hazel eyes—were wide open but unseeing.

He was dead. Rylan was dead.

"Rylan!" I sobbed, shooting up, soaked with sweat.

Darkness enveloped me. It wasn't real. It was a nightmare like no other I'd experienced before. This one was so real. So vivid. My heart was still hammering hard against my chest, and I was breathless. I stood from my bed, my body trembling, and peered out my bedroom window.

Rylan's bike was still parked in its usual space next door. Thank the gods.

There were two quick knocks at the door before the knob twisted and it opened.

"Eris, are you okay?" my dad asked, his brow furrowed with concern.

Camden poked his head in right behind him, sniffing the air, his eyes almost glowing gold.

"What are you doing?" I exhaled.

His narrowed eyes met mine. "Checking to make sure there isn't a dog in your room."

I growled at him. "There isn't. I just had a bad dream."

"About Rylan?" Camden asked with a raised brow.

"Yes. And it's not the kind of dream you're thinking of."

I proceeded to tell them about the nightmare and how real it felt.

"It could be a premonition," my dad said. "Your mother used to get them all the time. A foreseeing of the future."

"Did they ever come true?" I asked.

"Yes," he sighed. "She rarely got them, but every time she did, she'd wake up crying or screaming. They were burdensome for her. She didn't like that part of her gift."

I only needed to know one thing. "Can it be changed?"

"I don't know. I guess it's possible, depending on the circumstances."

"Just talk to him in the morning," Camden said, stretching his muscular arms over his head. "I'm going back to bed." He started walking away. "And please, don't yell a dude's name like that again. I was about to pounce in here and bite someone's head off."

"I love you, too!" I hollered after him.

"If you have any questions about the premonitions, maybe you should call your grandmother. She has them, too," my dad said softly.

I was shocked, but shouldn't have been. "I will. Thanks."

"Good night, sweetheart." My dad smiled and closed the door.

I fell back into my pillow and stared at the ceiling. The dream was probably triggered by the visit from a girl named Keira, who was a member of Rylan's old pack. Somehow, desperate and alone, she found him to tell him about a psycho shifter named Lars, who was hunting down and killing off the members of his old pack. There were only six left—of the twenty they originally had.

Rylan had told me a little about Lars. How he suspected he was the killer of both his parents, and now, he'd murdered their pack's current alpha, Axel. Rylan was their last hope . . . their only means of survival. They were running for their lives, and I'd overheard the girl, Keira, tell him those remaining members were in Montrose, over an hour away.

They'd been there for a few weeks now, while Rylan decided whether he wanted to take on the new role as their alpha. I knew he was conflicted. From what I knew about Rylan, after spending almost a month with him, he was torn. I could see it on his face and the way he stiffened after he had the discussion with Keira.

He'd grown up with them. They were his family, and I knew he wouldn't leave them out there alone to fend for themselves. Especially when that psycho was out there, murdering for whatever sick, twisted pleasure he got out of it.

I knew Rylan was going to leave. I just didn't know when.

I'd tried to talk to him after the Festival of Lights, but he was tight-lipped. He didn't want me or my family involved in his past issues. He wanted to deal with Lars alone.

After the dream . . . I was worried as hell. I had to find a way to convince Rylan that our pack, the Blaekthorn Shadow Pack, was his pack too. We were his family now, and any one of us would do anything to help him. But convincing him of that wouldn't be easy.

CHAPTER 2

RYLAN

*S*leep evaded me. I watched rays of moonlight stream through cracks in my curtains, one of them illuminating the new tiger's eye amulet Eris's dad had given me. An amulet like other members of the Blaekthorn Shadow Pack wore that kept them from being forced to change by the moon's phase.

Before Eris's mother died, she'd searched for the spell, and when she'd found it, she cast it over the stones so her family wouldn't have to live with the curse. She also planned ahead, spelling extra stones, knowing the family would inevitably grow.

Then, they eventually found Havenwood Falls. The town seemed to call to supernatural beings, drawing them in so they wouldn't have to be alone. Those who weren't completely human—like me.

In Havenwood Falls, the Court of the Sun and the Moon governed the supernatural residents. They had rules to ensure every supernatural being was able to control their gifts, and to keep the humans in the town safe. Each supernatural resident and visitor was given a tattoo, and the tattoo meant something different for each supernatural being. The Blaekthorns' tattoos allowed them to change at will, so within the town's wards, they didn't really need the amulets Eris's mother had spelled.

But should any of them leave the magical town, the amulets were a must. Which was why I wondered why Piers had given me one.

Maybe he knew I was about to leave.

Grasping the stone in my fingers, I couldn't help but wonder what my life would have been like if I hadn't wandered here and met Camden. And now, as fate would have it, I was part of the Blaekthorn Shadow Pack and family. A pack where Eris's father was alpha.

Seeing Keira a few weeks ago brought back every horror I'd tucked away—memories from the past that haunted me. And now the horrors were following me, just when I thought my life was taking a turn for the good.

Was I damned to live a life of running and fighting for my life? Because I was tired and didn't want to run anymore.

Hell, I wished I could close my eyes and have it all be a terrible nightmare. But it wasn't. Lars was out there—so close to my new home and the people who helped mend my shattered life. A life I thought was irreparable.

I couldn't let Lars set foot in this town, and wouldn't allow the Blaekthorns to get injured or killed trying to help me.

The bastard murdered both of my parents. And although we didn't witness him do it, we all knew it was him. His scent was always there, lingering around the gruesome scenes.

Lars had coveted everything my father had, especially my mother. He was infatuated with her, and believed she was supposed to have been *his* mate. When she refused him, he completely snapped and went on a killing spree, leaving nothing in his wake but chaos and bloodshed. Starting with my father.

Although I wanted to, I knew I couldn't ignore Keira's plea. It was an enormous weight pressing on my already heavily laden shoulders. A weight I never wanted to bear.

Hell, I was graduating high school in a few months and just wanted to start my life over. To work and have some semblance of a normal life. Was that too damned much to ask?

I now had a good life, with people who actually cared for me and took me in, who gave me a job and a roof over my head. I was thankful for them. They were a close-knit and loving family, and I knew they would do anything for each other. Which was why I didn't want any of my old pack's baggage to be dragged back here.

And then there was Eris, my half-witch, half-shifter girlfriend. She wanted me to open up and involve them in that part of my life. But it was too dark, and I knew she could get sucked up into that darkness if I let her in.

The burden was weighing heavier with each passing day, but there was only one right choice. I'd been avoiding for it too long already. I had to go. I had to leave Havenwood Falls and find Lars.

CHAPTER 3

ERIS

The sun had finally risen, and I was already dressed and ready to head over to Uncle Garrick and Aunt Vera's cottage. I had to let Rylan know about the dream. Maybe it could convince him to stay, or even ask for some help.

After being in Havenwood Falls for almost a month now with my childhood memories restored, I felt like I'd known the Blaekthorn Shadow Pack my entire life, even though I was still a newcomer to our pack. They were family, and they treated me no differently than they did Camden, who had never left. I knew they'd do anything for Rylan, now that he was also a part of the family.

I still couldn't get the nightmare out of my head. It was times like these I wished my mom were here to help me understand these new gifts. If she had premonitions, like my dad said, maybe she could have helped me understand them better. But since the Festival of Lights, I hadn't seen my glimmer—my secret ball of light that brought me so much hope and light whenever my world was dark. The light I found out was my mother, who had been with me all along.

Maybe she left because I was now old enough to stand on my own, and had found out the truth about her death. Maybe it was because I was back with the family in Havenwood Falls and had reconciled with my grandma.

I could call Grandma Gertie, but it was much too early in the morning. The last time I'd talked to her, when we went back to the house to pack up and move our things, she said she was actually considering moving to Havenwood Falls to be closer to me and Camden. But I knew she was torn. There was a gentleman back in New Mexico with whom she'd had a secret relationship, and he wasn't going anywhere.

I peeked out my window and saw Rylan's light click on. Then he opened his curtain and looked directly at me. I waved, and when he waved back, I signaled for him to come over. He acknowledged me with a nod.

My insides twisted in knots. When he disappeared and his light clicked off, I quietly made my way downstairs and threw on my jacket. It was the end of January and about twenty degrees outside.

Slipping outside, I closed the door, and when I turned around, Rylan was standing inches away. He grabbed my neck and pressed his warm lips to mine, stifling my scream.

"What the hell?" I exhaled, breathless. "How did you get here so quickly?"

His head cocked to the side. "I couldn't wait to see you."

"Mmm," I hummed, taking his hand in mine. "Can we take a walk?"

"Sure. Anything wrong?" he asked, his hazel eyes sweeping over me.

"No. I mean . . . I don't know." I looked into his eyes and couldn't help but flash back to the dream, and seeing those eyes without life, his throat ripped out, blood staining his face and the ground around him.

"C'mon, cupcake. Tell me what's on your mind." He tried to smile, but his eyes were studying me, like he knew something was wrong.

I let out a long exhale, my breath commingling with the cold air swirling in front of me. "I had a dream last night. But it wasn't a regular dream. It was different from any other dream I've had. It was so vivid and real, as if I were watching the event happen right in front of me."

His eyes narrowed, and a grin rose on his lips. I knew the dream I had was something totally different than what he was expecting, and it made my chest ache.

"What event were you watching?"

I paused, not sure if I wanted to tell him. But the reason why I couldn't go back to sleep and why we were standing out in the frigid cold this morning was that he needed to know.

"It was about Lars—he . . . he killed you." And although his expression changed to one of disappointment, I proceeded to tell him the entire dream, whether he wanted to hear it or not. Because maybe, just maybe, it could help save his life.

When I was done, Rylan didn't say a word. He stood there, quiet, his eyes staring blankly behind me.

"What are you thinking?" I breathed.

"I don't know," he replied.

I squeezed his hand and made him look at me. "Rylan, you aren't alone. We're—"

"No," he said, firmly. "You and your family are good people. I won't drag any of you into the tangled web that bastard is weaving. He may be a psycho, but he has a plan. It's been his plan since the beginning. To kill my father and his entire pack, including me. He's trying to prove he is stronger than any of us, and wants to punish us all. He thinks the reason my mother rejected him was because of the pack's influence. Like I said—he's a mental case. He believes he needs to fulfill this personal vendetta. And he won't stop until I and the rest of the pack are dead."

My stomach knotted. "Or unless he dies."

His eyes finally met mine, the gold rim around them more pronounced. "Yes. And that's what I plan to do."

It was selfish of me to ask, but I had to. "You don't have to go. You can stay here with me. You're safe here."

Those hazel eyes stared directly at me. "I wish that were true. But there is no safe place for me. Not yet. He'll keep searching until he finds me, and I don't want that bastard anywhere near you or your family."

"Rylan, you helped stop the witch who put Camden under the spell and tried to kill my dad. Let us help you. Please."

His eyes softened, and his arm wrapped around my waist, pulling me closer to him. "You have to understand. Lars gets off on the hunt and even more on the kill. He has no remorse. I won't put your family in danger, after all they've done for me." He wrapped his other arm around me, pulling me tight against his warm body, his calloused hand caressing my cheek. "Especially you. I don't want that bastard near you. I don't want him to know that you exist. Understand?"

I nodded.

Rylan leaned forward and kissed my forehead, then pressed his brow against mine. "I know you want to help, but I can't let you. If anything happened—" He didn't finish, but the sadness in his eyes spoke loud and clear.

There was nothing I could say or do to change his mind, so I remained quiet.

"Hey," he said, trying to break the tension. "I have to work for a few hours at the warehouse, but how about I pick you up for lunch? My treat." His cocky grin was back.

"Sure," I smiled back. "I'll see you then."

Rylan picked me up at noon in the company truck, since I was forbidden by practically the entire family to ride on his motorcycle while it was winter. He took me to Burger Bar, and the lunch crowd was bustling.

As we entered the restaurant, Rylan walked up to a tall, skinny guy with light brown hair, wearing jeans and a T-shirt.

"Hey, Jace," Rylan said, holding his hand out to him. "How are you holding up?"

The boy shook his hand and gave a dimpled smile. "Fine," he said, but his eyes said otherwise. He looked . . . sad.

"If you need anything, let me know," Rylan added, slapping a hand on his shoulder.

Jace nodded and gave a solemn smile. "Thank you. That means a lot."

When we walked away, I asked, "Who was that?"

"Remember the girl, Heidi Bennett, who went missing in December?"

"I remember you mentioning her."

"That's her boyfriend, Jace Edwards."

"Oh," I said, and suddenly felt bad for him. No wonder he looked so sad. He must have been battling his own demons.

As we passed by some of the booths, Rylan stopped again. I recognized one of the boys. It was Kase Kasun, with a few other boys I'd seen at the Festival of Lights a few weeks ago. Most likely football players, because Rylan greeted them with fist-bumps.

"Hey, Eris," Kase said with a tip of his head. "You should meet my sister, Willa. I heard you two have some things in common."

"Yeah, I'd like that." I remembered Rylan mentioning that Kase's twin sister, Willa, was a late shifter, too. And future alpha of her pack.

"I'll let her know. Maybe you and Rylan can come over for dinner sometime soon."

"Sounds good, man," Rylan said, grabbing hold of my hand.

I nodded. "Thank you."

Since I'd come to this town, I'd realized there were so many different species out there. I'd met a vampire, a dragon shifter, an angel, and much more. Havenwood Falls was a place of magic and monsters. Monsters like me and Rylan.

As Rylan pulled me past one of the booths, I spotted Julianna Fairchild, who was in a class I'd just started on Thursday nights at Sun and Moon Academy—an Awakening Lab for supes who had awakened but needed work honing their powers.

"Hi, Julianna," I said, waving. She was beautiful, smart, and voted Miss Teen Havenwood Falls. She was also fae. Her lavender hair was braided down her back and accessorized with a daisy.

Julianna waved back. "Hey, Eris. It's just Jules, remember?" She smiled, then introduced the girls at her booth. "This is Paisley, my cousin, and her friends, Taylor and Makenzie."

"I know Eris," Taylor said. "We, like, met at the clinic when Camden was admitted."

"Yes, we did. It's good to see you again."

Taylor smiled. "Totally."

"How is your brother?" Jules asked.

I smiled and nodded. "He's good. Back to normal, I guess. I'm still trying to figure him out."

"It must be hard," Paisley added, "to adjust."

"It is," I replied. "But it's been good . . . so far."

They all smiled, and Rylan cleared his throat.

"We'd better get a booth before they're all gone," I said. "I'll see you Thursday, Jules?"

"Yeah, see you."

We went inside and found an empty booth at the back, then ordered burgers, tater tots, and milkshakes.

Our time there was mostly quiet, and there was an unspoken tension in the air, knowing danger was close, and Rylan would eventually be going out to look for it. I tried to keep the conversation light, but every time I looked at him, the vision of him dead flashed in my mind.

"How's your burger?" he asked, shoving the last bite of his triple bacon cheeseburger into his mouth in record time.

"It's great," I said with a forced smile.

Rylan reached across the table and took my hand, his gold-rimmed hazel eyes fixed on mine. "Hey, don't worry about me."

"But that's the problem, Rylan. I do worry. Because I care."

His eyes shifted down to our connected hands. "I know. But you have to understand. I've been a loner most of my life, and opening up to someone like you . . . it's not easy for me. I've become a master at hiding my emotions and feelings, because out there, when your entire life is surviving, having feelings or emotions is weakness. So you're gonna have to cut me some slack."

"You're right. I don't know what it's like to live in fear every day, or to have to fend for myself. But I know, without a doubt, that if I ever had a problem or something bothering me, I could go to my dad and he would help me through it, whatever it was. Having someone to talk to is not weakness. It's strength. We are your family now, Rylan. We care about you. *I* care about you. And you have to cut me some slack for trying to make you understand my position. We are a family and a pack, and with that comes trust and strength in numbers."

Rylan let out a deep sigh, then ran his fingers through his thick brown hair. "There were twenty members of my old pack and now there are six. And, even now, it could be less. I would rather walk away now than to drag your family into this mess, knowing that if anything happened to them, their blood would stain my hands."

I closed my eyes. He wasn't getting it. I could see his point, but it seemed he wouldn't budge. My father and uncles had been around for a very long time, and kept very physically fit with their jobs. I knew if they met this rogue shifter, together they would be able to take him down.

"Hey, wanna go?" he asked.

I nodded and stood from my chair. There was no more I could say.

CHAPTER 4

RYLAN

J told Garrick and Vera I was going to spend the night hanging out with Kase and a few other boys from the Havenwood Falls High football team. I hated lying to them, but I had an overwhelming feeling that if Eris knew I was leaving, she'd send them after me.

I hated the look she gave me at the Burger Bar. She was pouring her heart out, trying to get me to open up and see her side, but I still felt like an outsider. I was still on probation, and now, some of my old pack's trash was being dragged back, leaving chaos in its path.

I was a lot bigger and stronger than any of the other male members of the pack, including my dad and Axel, who was my dad's best friend and the most recent alpha, until, as Kiera told me, Lars murdered him, too. I wanted to prove, not only to the Blaekthorns but to myself, that I was capable of taking care of this bastard alone. That I was stronger and smarter than him.

I had no real plan, but knew I needed to get as far away from Havenwood Falls as I could, as quickly as possible, and hopefully put an end to this once and for all.

It was after nine o'clock when I left. The sky was dark, and endless stars sparkled across it. It was a beautiful night despite the horror that lay within it . . . in Montrose.

The look on Eris's face when she told me about the nightmare she'd had was burned in my mind. She was truly concerned, and if premonition was one of her newfound gifts, I'd have to consider it.

Despite the patches of ice still on the roads, I hopped on my motorcycle. Knowing I would be leaving, I winterized it, buying studded tires and installing a windshield. It was my only source of transportation, so I'd have to take it.

The road conditions weren't too bad. Plus, with enhanced vision and reflexes, I maneuvered around the ice patches quite easily.

The road out of Havenwood Falls was quiet and dead. The only sound was the rumbling of my motorcycle and the whipping wind as I sped toward Montrose, and it took a little over an hour to get to the location Keira had written on the paper.

As I pulled into the parking lot of the motel, the hairs on my skin raised. I glanced around. The entire area was eerily similar to the scene Eris had dreamed about and described to me, as if she'd been here.

If she truly had a premonition, then Lars was already here, watching, waiting . . . stalking from the shadows. There were no humans around, and I didn't blame them. This entire area seemed like a slum, a place one would avoid even during the daytime.

I sniffed the air and couldn't catch a scent of anyone from my old pack. Maybe they'd moved on, knowing Lars was on their tail. Keeping my senses on full alert, I constantly scanned the dark areas.

I could feel the wolf inside me, raking its claws against my human skin, ready to break out at any given moment. It was begging to be set free. But I couldn't let it loose yet. I had to keep it inside until the time was right.

He was here. I could sense him, but I didn't want him to run.

If he was here . . . it needed to end here.

I kicked the stand on my bike down and slid off, aware of everything going on around me. Then I heard it. That deep, guttural growl.

The hunter was here, but I was fully aware. I had been given a warning ahead of time. A glimpse into the future. But this situation would have a much different outcome. I'd make sure of it.

Since Eris told me about her dream, I'd run this scenario through my mind a thousand times. I thought I would be more afraid, but as I stood under the starry, crescent-moon-lit sky in front of the motel, the only illumination a single flickering light, I had no fear in me at all. I could only describe what I felt as rage.

This bastard had taken everything from me. He murdered my parents in cold blood, and now he had the balls to hunt me?

I was no longer the helpless little boy he'd seen years ago. I was now in my prime, stronger than ever, and ready to take him on. Alpha or not. This prick would pay.

My skin was tingling, knowing he was so close. I knew where he was. Eris had told me, and his quiet growls confirmed it. He was to my left, downwind.

My girl had given me the upper hand.

The moon wasn't full, but Lars had shifted. I'd heard that he'd sought out dark witches. Maybe they'd given him a way to shift at will too.

I slowly slid from my black leather jacket and laid it on the seat.

The low rumbling from the beast was getting louder, and now, I could hear his claws scraping against the pavement.

I readied myself. I was bred for this. It was in my blood to protect my pack and fight for my life.

I turned to see two red eyes glaring at me.

Then a huge black wolf stepped out of the shadows, lips curled over razor-sharp teeth, foam frothed at the corners of its mouth. He crouched to an attack position, then . . . he charged.

I let the beast inside free and shifted, meeting him head on.

CHAPTER 5

ERIS

I'd just come home from a late dinner at Napoli's with my dad and Camden, when I noticed Rylan's bike was gone.

"Cam, do you know where Rylan went?" I questioned.

His eyes narrowed on me. "Why? Are you keeping a tight leash on him?"

"Camden," my dad said in his fatherly tone.

"No, Eris. I don't know where he is," he sighed. "Probably hanging out with some of the guys, like he did on the weekends before you came to town."

Having Camden in my life as a big brother was still an adjustment. And I could tell it was for him, too.

I had a sinking feeling Rylan wasn't with friends. I couldn't shake the feeling that he'd left and didn't tell anyone. Butterflies were slamming around in my gut, and they wouldn't stop. I had to find out where he was, that he was safe, to ease my mind.

When my dad stopped the car, I hopped out.

"I'm going to visit Aunt Vera," I said, already heading next door. Their kitchen light was on, and I saw a figure moving around inside. They were still awake.

"Sure you are!" Camden teased, and I heard my dad mumble a few words.

I knocked on the door, feeling breathless until Aunt Vera opened it.

"Eris! How are you doing, sweetheart? Come in," she said, grabbing my wrist and pulling me inside. It smelled like a bakery.

She immediately walked over to the stove, slipped on an oven mitt, and pulled out a sheet pan from the oven. "Would you care for a cinnamon roll?"

"I'd love one," I said, sitting at the table. I'd learned to never turn food down from either of my aunts when they offered it, because they would insist, and I'd get whatever it was anyway.

As she took a plate out of the cupboard, she turned to me. "Rylan isn't here, love. He went over to Kase's house to hang out for a while. You know, Sheriff Kasun's son."

"Okay. And yes, I know Kase," I said nonchalantly, trying not to raise my stress levels. But even after hearing her say he was with his friends, I still couldn't settle myself. I couldn't shake the feeling that he had left. I felt it in my bones. It was an uneasiness that wouldn't go away, even as my brain tried to push the thought away.

"So, how was dinner?" she asked, setting the hot cinnamon roll with gooey cream cheese frosting slathered over it and a cold glass of milk in front of me. I breathed in the scents of cinnamon and sugar, and it made my mouth water.

"We went to Napoli's. The restaurant was full, and the pizza was great."

"I love Napoli's. They do have the best pizza."

I agreed, glancing around. "Where's Uncle Garrick?"

"Oh, he's working late at the warehouse. There were a few big orders that came in for next week. He wanted to make sure they were all ready to go."

"Always working." I laughed.

"He is always working, but he loves it."

We chatted about shopping and my homeschool lessons while I

finished my dessert and milk. An hour later, I said goodbye, carrying a Tupperware of cinnamon rolls next door to my dad and brother.

Outside, the cold bit my nose and cheeks, and made my breath billow in front of me. I quickly ran toward the warmth of my house and slipped inside.

"Find what you were looking for?" my dad asked, sitting at the kitchen counter with some paperwork.

"Yes and no," I said, sliding the Tupperware next to him.

"What's this?" He peeked under the lid and took in a deep breath.

"Cinnamon rolls. Aunt Vera insisted."

"Is there one for me?" Camden piped in, standing at the top of the stairs.

"Yep. Knock yourself out."

He ran down the stairs, grabbed his roll and ran back up. "I'll tell her thanks in the morning."

I sat on a stool next to my dad.

"You're concerned," he said. He could read me like a book, even when I was trying not to look concerned.

"I think Rylan left Havenwood Falls."

The look on my dad's face showed genuine concern. "Your nightmare. Do you think he went after the shifter alone?"

"I do. He told me earlier today that he doesn't want any of us involved. He feels like this is all on him."

"Did he mention anything to Garrick or Vera?"

"Aunt Vera said he told her he was going to hang out with Sheriff Kasun's son, Kase, and some football boys."

My dad slid off his stool, headed to the phone, and dialed a number.

"Hey, Ric. This is Piers Blaekthorn . . . I'm great, thanks . . . Yes, Camden is doing well. If it weren't for you and the others finding and helping him, we probably would have lost him. Yeah . . . Thanks again . . . Hey, I wanted to ask if Rylan, the kid staying with Garrick and Vera, is with your son Kase?"

I waited, desperate to hear an answer.

"Okay, thanks . . . I'm not sure, but if there is, I'll be sure to let you know. . . All right. Thanks, Ric. I appreciate it . . . Bye."

It felt like forever when my dad hung up and finally gave me the answer. "Kase has been home all night. He's asleep on his dad's couch."

My heart sank. The feeling I'd had in my gut, since I saw his bike missing, was right. Now, hours had passed since he'd left. That meant he was already in Montrose, and . . . I couldn't think about it. I had to remain positive. He was still alive. I had no choice but to believe it.

"He should have talked to us. As a family, we could take care of one rogue shifter together," my dad said.

"I know. But he didn't want any of us to get hurt or killed. He was looking out for—"

"You. He was looking out for you," my dad murmured. "But still." He headed for the stairs. "He should have told one of us." My dad was in his alpha mode, protective.

"Where are you going?" I called after him.

"I'm going to get ready and call your uncles. We're going after him."

"I'm coming with you!" I hollered, making my way to the stairs.

My dad stopped at the top and glared down at me with a look that made me freeze in place. "You are not coming, Eris. You're staying right here with Camden and your aunts, where it's safe."

"Dad."

"Eris, don't argue with me. You're staying." He was using his voice of authority—the voice of our alpha. A voice I had no choice but to submit to.

So I kept my mouth shut and stormed to my room.

"I'll need his location," he said, before shutting his bedroom door.

The location. I didn't have a location. I didn't see the paper Keira had given him. But . . . the dream. In the dream I saw a sign—Montrose Mini Mart.

I quickly flipped opened my laptop and googled the location, then looked for the nearest motel. On the map, there was one motel nearby. I wrote the address down on a piece of paper, and when I heard my dad exit his room, I met him in the hall and handed it to him.

"There is a reason why Rylan didn't tell you he was leaving. A reason why he wants you to stay. I can't let you go, either. Not this time."

"I know." I knew he was right, but I still wanted to go.

"We'll find him," he said, then bounded down the stairs and out the door. I knew my dad and my uncles would be able to take care of themselves. I just hoped—with all my being—that they would make it in time to save Rylan.

Back in my room, I pulled out my Book of Shadows, the one passed down from my great-grandmother. I ran my fingers over the cover, and they tingled as they felt all those powerful spells within.

I wanted to learn all the spells. To master them, especially now that I knew there were other supernaturals in the world, and not all of them good. It was an advantage I was given.

As for the shifter part of me, I still hadn't made the change yet, but I knew it was coming. I could feel the wolf inside, growing in strength, getting ready to be set free.

I wondered when and how it would happen. Would it come with some kind of trigger? Maybe a life or death situation? Or would it happen randomly?

I hoped it wouldn't happen while I was in town shopping or around strangers. And hopefully the tattoo Addie Beaumont had given me when I first arrived would keep that from occurring.

Turning the pages, I came upon a spell—The Five Second Spell. This particular spell could freeze time around the caster for five seconds, and only the one who cast the spell would be able to move, while everyone else was frozen and unaware of anything going on.

The spell, in the wrong hands, could be dangerous. But in the right hands, five seconds could save a life. Or lives.

I memorized the spell and wondered if it would work.

"Hey, Eris," Camden called. "Have you seen my jacket?"

"It should be in the laundry room. On the dryer."

"It's not there," he hollered back. Then I realized I'd thrown it on when I went outside to check the mail this morning. It was lying over my chair. "Eris! I forgot I have to pick something up from the store. Could you please come down here and help me look for it."

I looked at the spell book and knew this would be the perfect time to try it out. I stepped out into the hallway holding the jacket behind my back and looked down to see Camden digging through the dryer in the laundry room.

I quickly recited the spell and . . . Camden stopped moving. He was frozen.

Holy crap! The spell worked!

I quickly tossed the jacket down, and it landed on the couch in the living room. Camden suddenly unfroze and smacked his head on the rim of the dryer.

"Dammit," he cursed as he rubbed the back of his head.

"Your jacket is right there on the couch," I said, pointing down at it.

"What?" He stood and looked at the couch, his brow furrowed. "It wasn't there a few seconds ago."

"Then it must have magically appeared," I said, shrugging.

Inside I was laughing, giddy the spell worked, and it made me want to learn more.

So to keep my mind from going insane until I heard word from my dad about Rylan, I stayed in my bedroom and went through the spell book, learning easy spells that might be helpful in the future.

Camden didn't show any signs of magic, and he was pretty sour about it. Maybe even a little jealous, and I didn't blame him. But my dad explained that in our family, the magic only seemed to pass to the women. He thought that maybe it was a spell by my great-great-grandmother, but he wasn't sure, and said my mom wasn't sure, either.

My stomach twisted inside, as I once again thought about Rylan. I hoped he was okay.

CHAPTER 6

RYLAN

*T*eeth and claws and fur collided in mid-air. Lars was strong, and his unhinged jaws and razor-sharp teeth seemed to be everywhere. He was relentless . . . but so was I.

Knowing what he did in Eris's dream, I kept my head down to block my neck. It seemed tearing out or slicing necks was his modus operandi.

Giant paws slammed into my side, ripping through skin, trying to push me back, but I was just as big and strong as he was. I rammed into him, using my head to push him back. He faltered a bit, allowing my claws to rake down his left shoulder, through fur and flesh.

Ducking, I dodged claws aimed for my cheek. As I turned away from him, he sunk his jaws into my right shoulder. Yelping, I sank my teeth into his back, thrashing my head from side to side until he howled in pain and his jaws unhooked.

As his head whipped back, I swiped my left paw against his face, aiming for his eye. I pushed my claws out, sinking deep into his eye socket. His eyeball burst, fluid spraying as I raked my razor-sharp claws downward.

Lars howled and backed away, part of his eye hanging like jelly. I went to strike again, but a car came down the road, headlights pointed in our direction.

While my attention wavered, Lars took off, running. This prick could not get away.

I gave chase, bounding after him, but he was faster than I'd thought. About a mile down the road, I lost him.

I stood in the middle of a four-way street and caught a faint scent of Lars on the breeze. But then I caught a new scent. An even stronger one—from members of my old pack.

I stopped and sniffed the cold wind. The scent was coming from the opposite direction where Lars had run. The coward. He'd finally met his match, but I knew it wouldn't be the last time I ran into him. He was power hungry and would come for revenge. But for now, I injured him. His healing powers couldn't give him a new eye, and he was now at a disadvantage, being partially blind. I'd go hunt for him after I made sure the others were still alive and safe.

Following their scents, I ended up at an old dilapidated shack that looked uninhabited. Before I approached, I raced back to my bike and shifted, changing into new clothes. I then slipped a gun into my pocket, one I'd had since I was young. It was my father's, and I'd only shot it a handful of times. In my human form, I'd need extra protection in case Lars returned.

Hopping on my bike, I headed back to the shack. As I neared it, I turned off the headlights and called out. "Keira? Keira, are you here?"

A few moments later, two figures exited. It was Keira and her mother Karina. They were dirty, their hair matted and clothes torn. They both ran up to me with tears streaming down their faces.

"Rylan. You came," Keira sobbed, her eyes wide with tears.

"I told you he'd come. I told you," her mom said, visibly shaken.

They looked like they hadn't eaten or bathed in days, so I reached in my pack and pulled out some water and a sandwich I'd made before I left. They gratefully took both, gobbling down the sandwich and drinking the water before saying another word.

"Where's the rest of the pack?" I asked, after I knew they could finally speak.

"Dead," Keira's mom replied, wiping a drip of water making its way down her chin. "We're all that's left."

I suddenly felt like shit. "I'm so sorry," I said, knowing those words weren't enough. "I should have come sooner."

"But you did come. And that's all that matters," Keira replied.

"Are you able to walk? There's a laundromat about a half mile up the road. I didn't see anyone inside, but they should have a bathroom where you can get cleaned up. I don't think Lars will show himself tonight, but if he does, I'll be ready." I held up the gun, and they both nodded.

I could tell they'd been through hell. I couldn't imagine what they had gone through to get to this point. I felt terrible, that since I'd left the pack with my mom and found Havenwood Falls, I'd lived well. Far from the life they had—a life of running and being scared shitless, not knowing when Lars would strike.

I hopped off my bike and pushed it, walking with them until we reached the laundromat. Sure enough, there was a bathroom at the back, and no one out this late.

"Go ahead," I said. "I'll stay here and keep watch."

"You're bleeding," Keira said, pointing at my right arm. Blood had soaked through my shirt. I didn't even notice until she'd pointed it out. It was from the bite Lars had given me on my right shoulder, and another one to my side, where his claws had raked my skin. I could feel the stinging, so I pulled my black leather jacket on to hide it all.

When they went into the laundromat, I took a better look at the wound. The bite marks were pretty deep, and would need attention. What worried me was the amount of blood I was losing. I had to find a way to stop it, but first, I needed to make sure they were safe.

I sniffed the air, but there was still no sign of Lars. When the girls returned, they looked a lot better. They'd cleaned their faces and braided their hair behind their backs. I gave them each an extra shirt I'd packed, not knowing how long I would be chasing Lars. They threw them on and tied them at the front, since they were large and baggy.

"Thank you," Karina said. Because Keira and I were the youngest in the pack, she'd had a part in raising me.

She put her arm around her daughter. They looked so much alike. They had the same caramel-colored skin, curly onyx hair, dark brown eyes, and tall, thin frames.

"You're welcome. There's a mini-mart another mile down the road. I'll give you some money to buy some food and whatever else you need, while I figure out what we're going to do next."

I had hoped there would be another male left, so he could possibly take over as alpha. Because it was just the two of them, I would have to rethink. Maybe they could live a life without a pack. Find a place where they could be safe, and live normal lives.

I couldn't take them back to Havenwood Falls while Lars was still alive. He'd track us all right back to the town and finish what he started. I wasn't going to allow that bastard anywhere near that town, even if it meant me not returning.

As much as I wanted to go back to the life I had, I couldn't. I wouldn't risk the Blaekthorns' lives or what they'd worked so hard to gain. I was all Keira and Karina had now, and felt I was responsible for them until they could make it on their own. It's what my father would have wanted me to do.

We walked to the mini-mart, my senses on full alert, but it seemed as if Lars was truly gone. He was probably trying to figure out what to do with the eyeball hanging out of its socket.

I gave Karina some money and told them to buy whatever they wanted while I sat on my bike and waited. Feeling a little light-headed, I knew we had to find a safe place soon, because I needed to bandage up my wounds and rest. And the motel wasn't exactly a safe place.

Eris was probably worried as shit by now. And the only freaking thing I was worried about was that she'd never forgive me. She'd tried to get me to open up, and I completely shut her down. Her family had taken me in, and I walked out. I wouldn't blame them for hating me.

I glanced at my watch, wondering how much longer Keira and Karina were going to take. Minute by minute, I was feeling weaker.

The corners of my vision were darkening, and I was still losing a lot of blood. It was dripping down my fingers and onto the pavement.

Then I took in a deep breath and caught his scent. Lars was back. He was back, and I was in no condition to fight him. I wasn't even sure I could shift.

I looked to the side of the mini-mart and saw one red glowing eye. Then he took a step out of the shadows, his snout soaked with blood and his marred eye patched, confirming he was able to shift at will.

His sharp teeth were bared. He knew he'd injured me, and now he was back for the kill. I reached in my pocket for the gun, but everything around me was a blur.

Keira and Karina exited the mini-mart. Their bag of groceries dropped, some fruit and drinks rolling out into the parking lot. Lars's head snapped toward them, and they froze.

"Get back inside!" I yelled, but they weren't moving. "Karina. Take Keira inside." It was the first time I'd used my alpha authority. Both of their eyes connected with mine. "Now." Karina nodded and pulled her daughter back inside.

Lars stepped out even farther. The hackles on his back were erect. "You're going to die, pup," he growled.

How the hell could I hear him? I was only connected to and could only hear the members of my own family and pack. Then I heard a wicked laugh. "You've no idea who you're up against. I ripped your father to shreds, slit your mother's throat, and in a moment, you will join them."

"Why? Who the hell made you God, to decide who lives and who dies?"

"Your father stole my birthright. I was rightful alpha," he snapped. "He was a fraud."

"You bastard. You don't know what the hell you're talking about!" I roared, trying to get off the bike, but the world around me was darkening and my legs tingling.

Another growl reverberated through the parking lot. "Ask your father. You'll be reunited with him soon enough."

He took another step toward me, crouched and ready to strike. I was ready to fight to the death and wouldn't give him the pleasure of taking my life so easily.

"See you in hell," Lars roared, rearing back to pounce at me.

Suddenly, tires screeched into the parking lot, then someone called my name. It sounded like Eris's father.

I turned to see a large black truck come to a halt and all three Blaekthorn men jump out. I could feel the strength of their pack—my pack—and when I turned back, Lars was gone.

Piers and Garrick were immediately at my side. Barney was checking the area, while Garrick helped me off the bike.

"What happened?" Piers asked.

"He was here," I breathed and lifted my finger to where Lars was crouched a moment earlier.

"Garrick, stay with him. I'll be back," Piers said, running to the side of the mini-mart and into the shadows. I knew he'd shifted because I felt that raw power of the pack's alpha vibrating through the air.

"Where are you hurt?" Garrick asked, and I pointed to my shoulder. It was an effort to stay awake and keep from blacking out.

He slid my jacket off and took a look at the wound, then let out a few expletives.

"Barney, run inside and get me some alcohol and bandages. As many as you can." Garrick turned his attention to me. "There are a couple of wounds that I'll need to cauterize immediately. Once we get the bleeding stopped, you should be able to heal a lot faster."

"Do it," I said. I'd suffered similar pain in my past. This was just another to add to my list. "There are two women inside. Survivors."

"We'll take care of them," Garrick said, pulling a hunting knife from his pocket before heading to the back of the vehicle. A few moments later, he returned carrying a blowtorch.

"Where'd you get that?" I questioned.

"We're outdoorsmen. This is a convenience," he replied with a wide grin.

Barney came back with the alcohol, so Garrick poured some over his knife and then over my wounds. I bit back a yelp as he told Barney about Keira and Karina. Barney said he saw them near the back of the store, so he went back inside to get them.

Garrick lit the blowtorch and started heating up his blade. When the blade was orange, he gave me a look.

I moaned. "Hey, no pain no gain, right?"

"Yeah, something like that," he said, holding my arm firmly. "This is gonna hurt."

"I know. Do it before—"

He pressed the searing blade to my wound, and a growl ripped from my throat. It sizzled, burning and melting my flesh. A few moments felt like an eternity before he finally lifted the blade.

"The bleeding stopped on this wound. One down, one to go," Garrick said, pouring more alcohol over the knife to clean off the blood. "You still with me?"

I nodded, trying to catch my breath.

Barney came out with Keira and Karina, and they stood in front of us, watching.

"This next wound looks a little deeper." He made Barney press a cloth to the wound while he heated the blade.

The loss of blood already had me weak, to the point of passing out, and I felt like one more scorching blade to my shoulder would do me in. I sucked in deep breaths, trying to stay focused and coherent, when Piers finally returned.

"He's gone," he said. "I tracked him a few miles down, but the wind shifted, and I lost his scent. That bastard must have been moving."

"He'd better, with the Blaekthorn brothers on his trail." Barney laughed.

Piers laid a palm on my left shoulder. "Hang in there, Rylan." I could only nod, trying to keep the pain at bay. "Eris is the reason we're here," he continued, probably trying to divert my attention. "And by the looks of it, we came just in time."

I nodded again, and a smile lifted on my lips. Eris. I knew she would send them. I just hoped she wasn't too upset that I left without telling her.

Pain! Skin sizzled and melted together under the red-hot blade, cauterizing the wound. I was panting now, trying to keep in the moment. But it was too much.

"He's fading," Garrick's voice said, as darkness overcame me.

CHAPTER 7

ERIS

I nearly tripped down the stairs when the house phone rang. Cell phones had no service in our area of town, so we relied on our landline.

"Dad?" I puffed, knowing he would be the only one calling this late.

"We're on our way home," he said, like he would on any normal call.

"What about Rylan?" That was the one question hammering my mind for the past few hours.

"He's with us. We're all fine, but he's unconscious from a bite wound. It shouldn't be fatal. Your Uncle Garrick cauterized the ones that weren't healing quickly enough. We'll have to monitor him tonight."

"What about Lars? The other shifter?"

"He got away. But we have two survivors, a girl and her mother, whom we're bringing home with us."

I wondered if it was the girl Keira, and if Rylan knew if my dad and uncles were bringing them. He'd told me he didn't want them in Havenwood Falls, because he knew they would draw Lars here, too.

"Where will they stay?" I questioned.

"Tonight, they'll be staying with us. Get some extra blankets from the closet, and some clothes. They can stay in the living room tonight, and I'll figure out other accommodations for them in the morning."

"Sure. I'm on it."

I was just glad they were all safe and on their way back.

CAMDEN CAME HOME RIGHT as I was setting up the living room.

"Sleepover?" he teased as he walked through the door. But his smile dropped and his emotions shifted when he saw my expression.

"Dad found Rylan. He's injured."

"Where is he?"

"He was in Montrose. Dad, Uncle Garrick, and Uncle Barney are with him. They're on their way back now, but are also bringing two members of his old pack. I think it's the girl who met him at the Festival of Lights and her mother."

He nodded slowly. "How bad is his injury?"

"I don't know. Dad said he was bitten and a few of the wounds needed to be cauterized."

"Need help with anything?"

"No. But thanks."

"Okay," he replied. "I'll be in my room. Let me know when they arrive."

"I will." I watched Camden bound up the stairs. It was so odd, after all these years, to finally have a big brother I had forgotten about. But even after all those lost years, we seemed to have fallen effortlessly into our family roles, just as if we had been together since the beginning.

Camden was everything I thought a big brother would be like. Yes, he was protective, but he was also caring and still very sorry for the past and wanting our mother to live, rather than me. And I could tell he was trying to make up for it.

After setting up the bedding in the living room, I paced back and forth and up and down the stairs. It was driving me crazy not knowing how injured Rylan was, or how it happened. As soon as I heard tires on the gravel drive outside, I called up to Camden then ran out into the cold without a jacket. A wall of frigid air slammed into me, but I didn't care. I had to see him.

Uncle Garrick exited the front passenger seat first, and gave me a sad smile. "He'll be okay, but he'll need rest and time to heal."

I exhaled a bit of the building stress as the rear door opened.

Keira was the first to exit, and then an older woman who looked just like her slid out. Uncle Barney hopped out, and he and Uncle Garrick stood on each side of the passenger door. My eyes remained fixed into the dark space, waiting.

Then a soft moan exited the vehicle before he did. Rylan slowly slid out and looked at me, his hazel eyes filled with pain and . . . remorse. He was covered in blood—so much blood. It was smeared on his face and hands and had soaked through his shirt.

I wanted to run over to help, but Uncle Garrick took his left arm and Uncle Barney put a hand on his back for support. He cringed as he took a step.

"If he needs someone to look after him," Camden said from behind me, "I can stay over. Just to make sure he's still breathing in the morning."

"You sure?" Garrick asked.

"Yeah, he helped save me. It's the least I can do."

"Eris, why don't you show the ladies inside," my dad said. "It's awfully cold."

I'd totally forgotten about them standing off to the side.

"Come inside," I said, waving them forward.

They looked at each other first before following me in. I gave Rylan one last glance before I went inside, and he, in turn, gave me a pained grin.

"Keira, right?" I said, extending my hand.

"Yes," she answered, taking mine. "Thank you." She turned to the woman. "This is my mom, Karina."

I shook Karina's hand. "It's nice to meet you. Please, make yourselves at home." I pointed them to the bathroom, where there were clean towels and toiletries set up for them to shower. They were both a little taller than me, but they looked the same size, so I handed them each some new pajamas Aunt Vera had given me, along with some new undergarments. "These should fit. At least until we can get you to town to get some better ones."

"These will be wonderful," Karina said.

"There are food and drinks in the fridge and cupboard. Please, help yourself. We have more than enough." The two of them looked at each other with tears in their eyes. How long had they been on the run? How long had they been out in the cold without a shower, or food, or drink? Things that we didn't pay much mind to were so precious to them.

"You go first, Mom," Keira said, pointing to the bathroom. She nodded and smiled, wiping a stray tear trickling down her cheek.

"Good night, guys," Uncle Barney said loudly. "I'm outta here. Aunt Lydia will bust my balls if I don't get home soon."

Camden ran in and up the stairs. "Gonna grab some clothes."

I peeked outside and watched Garrick and Rylan slowly making their way toward their cabin, Rylan obviously in a lot of pain.

"Did you guys give him pain medicine?" I hollered after them.

"No," Uncle Garrick replied. "He knocked out before we could give him anything."

I headed to the medicine cabinet and found a bottle of extra strength Tylenol, then grabbed a bottle of water and ran out the door after them. I felt like I needed to help, even if it was only offering him pills.

They were almost to their front porch when I reached them. "I have pain meds."

"I'll take six," Rylan said with a grin.

"But . . . six isn't healthy," I said.

"Eris, he doesn't give a damn about his liver right now." Camden chuckled, coming up behind them. "He's in pain. Besides, he's a wolf with a very high metabolism. His kidneys will be fine."

I shook six pills out from the bottle and handed them to Rylan.

His hand was covered in blood, and I wasn't sure if it was his or the other guy's.

He gulped them down with the entire bottle of water.

"Thanks," he said, wiping a drip on his chin. His eyes lingered on mine, and I knew he wanted to talk.

"Tomorrow," I whispered. "After you've rested."

He nodded.

"Ry, you totally need to shower. You look like you've been in a mass murder," Camden jested.

Rylan gave a slight grin. "At least I took the guy's eye out."

"No way," Camden said.

"Yeah, I sunk my claws into his socket and the freaking eyeball burst. Eye juice splattered and eye jelly was hanging down the side of his face."

"Oh, God," I coughed, gagging as I pictured the scene.

Camden laughed. "Dude, that's messed up."

"Yeah, it was disturbingly brutal, but it felt great. And it was payback for the bastard biting me," Rylan coughed. "He would have killed me, but the cavalry came just in time." Rylan glanced at Garrick. "Thanks, again."

"Eris is the one you should be thanking," he said. "It was her premonition and gut feeling that led us to you."

Rylan's gaze turned to me, his expression telling me how thankful he was.

"Hey, Eris," Camden said, before opening the door.

"Yeah?"

"If he needs to be bandaged, I'll call you."

I laughed and turned back toward my house. "Fine."

When I walked in, Keira was hugging her pajamas. She looked so lost and sad and probably didn't have many friends, if any. Maybe I'd take them shopping tomorrow. They both needed some new clothes and winter jackets, so maybe we could head over to Backwoods Sport & Ski. The Kasuns—another pack of wolf shifters in town—owned the shop, so I could probably introduce them.

When Karina exited the bathroom, my dad approached her.

"Tomorrow, I'll have to take you both to get registered. It's something we nonhumans have to do in this town. And you'll each be given a temporary tattoo. It doesn't hurt, but you will be able to control your shifting at will."

"Really?" Keira's voice went up an octave, her eyes wide. "Shifting at will?"

"Yes, at least while you're staying here in the town."

"Okay."

"If you need anything, please let us know," my dad added.

"You're very kind," Karina said, bowing her head.

"Good night, everyone," my dad said, before heading up the stairs and disappearing into his room.

Keira slipped into the bathroom, while Karina got settled into bed.

Inside my room, I felt the stress over Rylan's safety melt away. At least he was here now, and he was safe.

CHAPTER 8

ERIS

The warmth of the sun shining through my window woke me. Glancing at the time, I saw it was eight o'clock. I guess Rylan didn't need help changing his bandages. After changing into jeans and a long-sleeved tee, I threw on a gray hoodie and decided to head downstairs to cook some breakfast.

As soon as I opened the door, I smelled food and heard voices. Aunt Vera and Aunt Lydia were already here, and by the smell, they'd probably whipped up a breakfast to die for.

Heading down the stairs, I noticed the kitchen counter filled with all kinds of breakfast food.

"Good morning, Eris," Aunt Lydia said, with a bright red apron and lipstick on. She and Aunt Vera looked like they could be on the cover of some cooking magazine. How on earth could they look so good this early in the morning? It was a miracle I'd managed to brush my teeth and get my hair untangled.

Karina and Keira were sitting at the table, chatting and laughing.

"Good morning," I said, waving to them.

"Good morning," they replied in unison.

"When did you guys get here?" I asked my aunts. I didn't hear them come in, let alone cook all this food.

"About an hour ago. Your dad called and said the girls were up, so we decided to welcome them with breakfast. Come and eat."

The table was filled with pancakes, sausages, bacon, hash browns, cinnamon rolls, and muffins. Hot coffee steamed from the French press, so that was the first place I went.

"Where's my dad?" I asked.

"He ate and took off. He said he had some work to do at the warehouse, and then he had a meeting with Sheriff Kasun and the Court to discuss the matter about the other shifter."

"Oh, okay," I said, snagging a chocolate muffin and some bacon. My dad had always been thorough. He never procrastinated. He did whatever needed to be done as soon as he could.

"He said he'll be back in a few hours to take Keira and Karina to register and get their tattoos," Aunt Lydia added.

"Hey, Eris, could you run over to my place and see if Camden is up? I tried calling, but it went straight to his answering service. His phone might be dead. If he is, tell him to come and eat before the food gets cold," Aunt Vera suggested.

"Sure." I was eager to check on Rylan anyway.

My heart pattered as I stood outside of Rylan's door. I quickly rapped twice and waited. When there was no answer, I slowly opened the door and peeked inside. Camden wasn't on the floor, so I swung the door open a little wider to see Rylan on his bed, lying on his back.

I looked down the hall and noticed the bathroom door was shut, so Cam must have gone inside. He'd be there for a while, so I decided to go in and check on Rylan.

His shirt was off, revealing his muscular arms, chest, and abs. The blanket covered his navel and everything below. I stepped in and tiptoed over to where he was. The bandage was off and lying on the floor next to his bed. Most of the smaller wounds had already healed. The larger ones were still visible, but the skin was connecting. Then, I noticed one wound that looked like Uncle Garrick had cauterized it. It was bright red and swollen.

I automatically reached over and gently rubbed my fingertips over the skin. It was hot.

"Couldn't wait to get your hands on me, cupcake?" Rylan whispered.

I gasped and snapped my hand back, then saw that crooked grin. That smirk I'd grown to love.

"Yeah, something like that," I exhaled, narrowing my eyes. "I thought you were sleeping."

"I was . . . until you touched me," he said. "I thought I was dreaming." He reached out and grabbed my hand. "I know you're probably pissed that I left without telling you. I'm really sorry."

"Don't," I breathed.

"No, I have to say this," he said, gently squeezing my fingers. "You were right. I should have told you. If I had, Lars would probably be dead, and I wouldn't be injured. But this is what I wanted to avoid happening to your family."

I was upset he didn't tell me, but not enough. I did see his side. He was looking out for me. And my family. "I know. And I forgive you."

"You do?" His eyes narrowed as if he thought I was going to fight him.

"I'm worried about this wound," I said, pointing to the area. "The scar tissue from the cauterization, and the surrounding area is swollen. It's bright red and hot. I think it's infected."

He tried to sit up, but plopped back down with a groan. He was still in pain. "I think I need more pills and water."

Sweat had beaded on his head, so I placed my hand to his forehead. "You have a fever. I think you should go to the clinic."

"No," he said quickly. "I just need rest. The injury is taking a bit longer to heal because it was more severe than the others."

"Then I'm going to get a second opinion."

"Can you come closer?" he whispered, tugging on my hand. "I have something important to tell you."

I took a step closer, until my legs were touching the bed, and bent over to hear what he had to say. His hand disconnected from mine, and in a flash was behind my neck, pulling me closer.

"Rylan," I breathed, but didn't fight it. I'd wanted to kiss him since the moment he returned.

His warm lips met mine, his breath sweet and minty. His fingers gently tangled in my hair, pushing me closer. His kiss deepened. His gentle touch, the way his tongue danced along my lips and raked across my teeth—even injured, he was setting me on fire.

"Well, that's some wake-up call," Cam snickered, making me gasp and pull back.

Damn him.

Rylan smiled and took my hand. "I was just wishing Eris a good morning," he replied.

"Yeah, sure." Cam threw on a T-shirt.

"Aunt Vera and Aunt Lydia cooked a huge breakfast next door. They sent me over to tell you the food is ready and you'd better hurry if you want it warm."

"I'm there." Camden stopped at the door. "Please, no making out until I leave the house," he said, then disappeared.

I turned back to Rylan, and he pulled me back down for one more breathless kiss.

"You're trying to distract me," I breathed, my head spinning.

"Is it working?" Another sly grin.

"No," I said, walking toward the door. "Stay here and . . . maybe put on a shirt." My eyes raked down his chest to his abs, and for a split second, I wanted to see what was below the blanket.

Rylan's hand went to the blanket, and my face immediately heated. "You're welcome to join me," he purred.

I backed up a little farther. "Tempting. But I'm going to go now, and get that second opinion."

"I THINK we need to get him to the clinic. This is infected, and I'm not sure why. He should be healing," Aunt Vera said, looking at the area. Rylan had thrown on a tank top, and I was thankful. "Let me make a call and see if someone can see him."

"No, it's fine."

"Rylan Gilles, you are living under our roof and under our care," she said in a motherly tone.

"Yes, ma'am," he replied.

A few minutes later, she came back. "The clinic is empty right now and Dr. Underwood just came in—that nice man who cared for Camden. So get ready. I'm driving."

Aunt Vera drove, and I sat in the back of her Expedition with Rylan. His face was a little pale, and he was still sweating, even though the air was icy cold.

Inside the clinic, Aunt Vera checked in while we waited.

"Room two, Rylan," she announced.

He stood.

"Do you want me to come with you?" I asked.

A grin. "If you want to. I'll probably have to take my shirt off again."

"Can't you just answer with a yes or no?"

He chuckled. "Come with me, cupcake."

"Fine," I exhaled, and grabbed hold of his hand.

We didn't wait long before Dr. Underwood came in wearing a white lab coat. He greeted us with a firm handshake and a smile.

"What's going on, Rylan?" the doctor asked, standing in front of him.

"I got into a tussle with another shifter, outside of Havenwood Falls," he answered. "My injuries are healing, except one. We think it might be infected."

"All right. I'll need you to remove your shirt so I can take a look."

While the doctor turned his back to put some gloves on, Rylan gave me a sexy side-eyed glance, and a wink, which made my stomach turn and my cheeks blush. I rolled my eyes, but kept them on him as he pulled his shirt over his head with his uninjured arm.

The doctor stepped up to him and held his hand over the infected area.

"There is something beneath the skin that shouldn't be there. That's why it won't heal and why there is an infection. I'll need to make a small incision to extract it."

Dr. Underwood was good. My aunt told me he was fae, so seeing him diagnose what was wrong without even touching Rylan had me in awe.

"Do you know what it is?" I asked.

He turned to me and shook his head. "I won't know until I get in there."

He went to the cabinet and brought back a few things. After dipping a cotton ball into a solution, he rubbed it across Rylan's shoulder.

"This is to disinfect the area," he said, then brought out a small needle. "And this is to numb the area."

He shot liquid into a few areas, and Rylan didn't even flinch. While we waited, he gathered a small incision knife and a long tweezer-like instrument.

He had Rylan lay back, as the wound was near his collarbone. Then he made a small incision, about an inch long. Using the tweezer thing, he reached in and pulled something out, dropping it into a cup filled with solution. He used a few butterfly closures to seal the wound, then placed gauze and held it down with some tape.

Dr. Underwood held up the cup and inspected what he had extracted.

His navy-blue eyes shifted to Rylan. "It looks like a tooth."

CHAPTER 9

RYLAN

a tooth? That bastard's freaking tooth was inside of me?

"Hey, Doc," I said, wondering if he could help make sense of something bothering me. "Is it possible to run a DNA test on that tooth?"

His eyes narrowed and so did Eris's.

"Is there something you'd like to find out?" Dr. Underwood asked.

"Yes, I want to find out if the owner of that tooth is somehow . . . related to me."

"Rylan," Eris breathed, questions swirling in her eyes. "Who do you think he is?"

"I don't know, but he said something to me last night that made me think."

"It is possible to take a DNA sample from a tooth," Dr. Underwood replied. "But I'll need to take a blood sample from you as well. I could have the results back in a day or two."

"That's perfect. Thank you, doctor."

The thought of Lars being related to me soured my stomach.

My father never had any brothers, or never mentioned any. I was born when my grandfather was alpha and was there when he died and my father gained his position.

I just needed to know. I wanted to find out why he would say those things to me . . . that he should have been alpha. Ever since I'd heard those words, my mind had become a whirlwind. There had to be more. A true motive behind all the murderous bloodshed. He was settling a personal vendetta, and I needed to find out the reason why.

After we left the clinic, Eris was quiet on the ride home. I knew her mind was spinning just as much as mine was, but I didn't want to talk while her aunt was in the vehicle.

As she pulled home and exited the car, I grabbed hold of Eris's hand.

"Can we talk?" I whispered.

She nodded, so I led her to the back of the cabins, where the family had built a greenhouse filled with flowers and vegetables. Inside, the greenhouse was warm. Red and white poinsettias were in full bloom.

As we walked down the center aisle, filled with flowers, Eris stopped me.

"Talk to me, Rylan."

I'd been so accustomed to shutting down, quenching all feelings inside to survive. But she, this girl whom fate had brought into my life, was demanding I open up. This was new for me, but I supposed it was a good thing. Because she was good, and was slowly chipping away at my calloused heart.

I wrapped my good arm around her and pulled her against me, because whenever she was close, I felt a little stronger. A little more . . . whole. She didn't pull or back away from me, so I looked deep into her beautiful golden eyes.

"First of all . . . I haven't properly thanked you."

Her eyes narrowed. "For what?"

"Your dream. Or nightmare. It was real. The details you gave me were so eerily similar to the area I was in, I couldn't help but believe everything else. The sign. The motel. The flickering light in the parking lot, and . . . Lars, standing downwind in the shadows. It all happened just like you said." I felt a pang of sadness as I thought of my mother. "I had to believe, because my mother also had the gift of premonition. She had dreamed of this place. And when she died, I followed that dream. It led me here, to Havenwood Falls." I cupped her face in my hands. "It led me to you." I pressed a kiss on her soft, sweet lips.

She stood there, eyes closed, and when they opened, she smiled. I ran my fingers down her soft cheek.

"Because of you, I'm standing here right now." A tear trickled down her face, and I wiped it away.

"What did that monster say to make you consider a DNA test?"

I knew she'd ask, and I decided I wasn't going to hide anything from her anymore.

"He told me that my father stole his birthright. And that he should have been alpha."

Eris shook her head. "That means he has to be related to you . . . to your father."

"I don't know. My father didn't have any siblings. He never mentioned any and neither did my mom. Or my grandparents. Maybe he's just insane. There is a reason why he is alone and not part of a pack. Rogue shifters have reputations for being wild and brutal, and I know that my father was the only one who had right to be alpha."

Eris plucked a flower from one of the pots and ran her fingers against the soft petals. "So, when did Lars show up?"

I had to think back. "After my grandfather died. It was a few weeks after my dad had become alpha. Like I told you before, our pack was one of the strongest, and targeted by rival packs. He claimed he was stronger and should take over. He also claimed he was in love with my mom, but how the hell did he even know her?" The last part I whispered to myself. But it was a good question. How the hell could he love someone he never knew?

"Was he stalking her?"

I thought back to the one time I'd remembered Lars coming into our camp and confronting my father. "The way he and my father talked, it was like they knew each other. And my mother. Lars held out his hand to her, begging for her to come to him. But her only reply was to stand next to my father and take hold of his hand, showing where her loyalty lay. With my father. In the hands of her husband and her alpha.

"That's when I saw the fury in his eyes. The same fury he had when he looked at me that night." I closed my eyes. "He called my father a fraud."

Eris ran her hand down my arm, sending a wave of goose bumps in her wake. "Rylan, are you sure you want to find out who this man is?"

I looked deep into her eyes and asked myself the same question.

"I want to know the truth," I finally admitted. "I need to know if my father was rightful alpha, and why this psycho would claim he was."

Then it was Eris who took my face into her soft, warm hands. "I am here for you, no matter what the report says."

"I know you are," I murmured, kissing her deeply. This girl. This half witch, half shifter who was still trying to find her place in the world, was trying her best to help me, the damaged shifter.

Fate led me to her. I knew it from the first moment I saw her standing in the doorway of the medical clinic. It felt as if her soul called to me, and every molecule in my body answered. I'd never felt more settled. She did that to me. She slowly filled that deep, dark emptiness in my chest with her light.

But with Lars still out there, I had to be extra careful. I would protect her at all costs. And, if it came down to it, I would give my life for her.

CHAPTER 10

ERIS

My dad came home and called a family meeting. He said he'd shared the information about the encounter with Lars with Sheriff Kasun and also with a woman at the Court of the Sun and the Moon. She said she would let the others know.

"All right, I have to take Keira and Karina to register and get their tattoos with Addie. They will be staying with us until we can find them a safe place of their own." My dad looked at Karina, and she nodded, placing a hand over her heart.

"Thank you."

I pulled my dad to the side. "Hey, do you think I can come with you? I'd like to take them to Backwoods Sport & Ski after to get them each a jacket and maybe a few warm things."

My dad wrapped his arms around me. "I'm proud of the woman you're becoming," he said. Then he slipped his credit card in my hand. "Get whatever they need to make them feel comfortable."

"You're the best," I said, hugging him tightly.

"No, you are. Now, let's get moving."

"Always the alpha."

"Always," he laughed.

"I'm gonna head over to my own bed and crash the rest of the day," Rylan said.

"Good," Cam replied. "Because I'm gonna crash on my bed for the rest of the day too."

xxx

The registration and the tattoos were done in less than an hour, and then my dad drove us to Backwoods Sport & Ski.

"This is a quaint town," Karina said. "So much charm."

"It is," I said. "My dad and I recently moved here, too."

"You did? It seems as if you've lived here for a long time."

"Well, it's complicated," I said, and saw my dad's eyes examining me in the rearview mirror. "I'll share the story another time."

Karina smiled. "Sounds good."

My dad pulled up in front of the store and let us out. "I've got to meet with a client about an upcoming order, and then was given the task of picking up dinner at Pyntz Butcher Shoppe. I'll pick you ladies up in an hour?"

"Sure," I said. "How about getting us at Coffee Haven."

"Fine. Go ahead and feed that caffeine addiction."

"Thanks, Dad." I slid out of the vehicle. "Let's go, ladies!"

"Where are we going?" Keira asked.

"Shopping," I said with a smile.

It took a while for me to convince Karina to pick something out, but when I told her that Keira and I would have to choose for her, she buckled.

They each got one warm jacket and enough shirts and pants to last a week. I even talked them into getting some new shoes, as their old ones had holes and weren't fit for the winter weather. Or walking, for that matter.

As we made our way to the register, I noticed how pale Keira had become, as if she'd seen a ghost. Her eyes were wide and frozen outside the window. When I turned to look, a man in a dark, hooded overcoat quickly turned and walked away.

"Keira, who was that?" I asked, but she didn't answer. She was trembling.

Meanwhile, Karina was looking at activity brochures the store offered.

"Hey, is she okay?" the girl behind the register asked. She looked so familiar, with dark, chin-length hair. She was wearing jeans, a T-shirt, and a fleece jacket with the Backwoods Sport & Ski logo on the front.

"Are you Willa Kasun?" I asked.

"I am," she answered with a smile.

"Nice to finally meet you," I said. "I met your brother, Kase."

"Oh, unfortunately," she giggled. "He's my twin brother."

"That's why you looked familiar."

Her brown eyes darted to Keira with concern. "Hey, does your friend need something? Water? A seat?"

I looked at Keira. Her eyes were still focused on the window.

"Karina, I think something is wrong with Keira," I said softly, trying not to make a scene. There were a few visitors in the store.

She walked over and grabbed her daughter's hand. "Keira, what's wrong?"

Keira's attention finally snapped to her mother. "I thought I saw a ghost."

"Oh," Willa chimed in. "And it won't be your last, here in Havenwood Falls. There are quite a few of them lingering about."

"No kidding." I laughed, knowing exactly what she meant.

Karina pulled Keira to the side and spoke quietly with her while I paid.

"You're new here?" Willa asked, swiping the card.

"Yes." I extended a hand to her. "I'm Eris Blaekthorn."

"Blaekthorn? You're Camden's sister?"

"Yes."

"How is he? I heard about the . . . incident."

"Yeah," I sighed. "He's alive and kicking and very snarky."

Willa chuckled. "So he's back to his old self."

"Yep."

She handed me the receipt and the bags. "It was nice to meet you,

Eris." She leaned in and whispered, "Kase told me you haven't shifted yet. If you want to talk sometime, just give me a call."

"I will. Thank you." She handed me a business card. "I guess I'll be seeing you around."

"I'm sure you will."

Outside, I handed Keira and Karina their jackets and they slipped into them.

"How about we go and get something hot to drink?" I pointed to Coffee Haven. "I think we all need some caffeine."

"Do they have tea?" Karina asked.

"They do."

As soon as I stepped into the coffee shop, I took in a deep breath. Heaven. It smelled like heaven.

We found an empty table at the back, then I got their orders and stood in line. I was desperate to know why Keira was so affected by the guy she'd seen.

Back at the table, I handed them their drinks, and Keira was still visibly shaken. "Hey, Keira. Are you all right?"

She nodded but stayed silent, her hands wrapped around her drink.

"Did you recognize the guy who walked past the window?" I asked bluntly. I didn't want to be left in the dark, especially when my family and I were a part of their lives.

Keira nodded. "I swear it was someone from our pack, but he's dead. We saw his body."

"Whose body?" I questioned.

"Axel's."

The breath caught in my throat. "The last alpha of your pack?"

She nodded.

Axel was Rylan's father's best friend, and the one who took over as alpha after he died.

I took Keira by the hand. "Are you sure it was him?"

She shrugged. "It looked exactly like him. He stared right at me."

"But he's dead, Keira. We saw his body," Karina said.

"How do we know it was his body? It didn't have a head."

"But it was his clothes, and he was wearing the ring."

"You know how easy it would be to plant a body and fake a death, especially if the body is headless? It could have been anyone."

Karina closed her eyes and rubbed her temples. "This is too much. I don't know what to think anymore."

I felt the same way, and couldn't wait for my dad to come and pick us up. Would this madness ever end? There were so many questions blasting in my mind, but one had me frightened.

"Hey," I whispered. "What if Axel got away and Lars faked his death to terrify the pack? And, if Axel is here . . . what if Lars followed him? What if Lars is already here too?"

"Gods no," Karina exhaled.

The mystery was plunging deeper and deeper.

When my dad finally pulled up, I told him everything that had happened. He was our protector and needed to know. On our way home, he had Keira describe what Axel looked like, and then called his brothers for a family meeting.

"Dad, I'm going next door to tell Rylan. He needs to know."

He nodded. "There's a meeting at our place in an hour. I want everyone there. If there is a threat already in the town, we have to cover all of our bases and make sure everyone is safe."

"Okay," I said, then ran next door.

Aunt Vera's and Uncle Garrick's cars were gone, so I lifted the wolf statue on the porch and took the spare key.

Inside, I ran upstairs to Rylan's room and knocked on the door. When he didn't answer, I slowly turned the knob and cracked the door open. His blackout curtains were drawn, making the room completely dark. I couldn't see anything beyond the threshold.

"Rylan," I whispered. "Rylan?"

I pushed the door open further and gasped when I saw golden-rimmed eyes close by.

A hand grabbed my wrist and yanked me inside. Lips crashed against mine as I was flipped onto the bed, and a large, warm body pressed on top of me.

"You dare come into my lair and wake me?" Rylan purred, his tongue swirling against my neck.

Oh, God. He was trouble. So much trouble.

"Rylan, I have to tell you something," I breathed.

"You know how long I've waited to get you alone?" His hands were everywhere, his teeth nipping at my ear and down my neck, extracting a moan. His breath was heavy, his body hot. So hot.

My fingers trailed up his muscular back and tangled in his hair. I wanted him so badly. Wanted his lips, his tongue, his mouth.

As if Rylan heard my thoughts, his mouth crashed down on mine, slow and sensual. I arched into him, and he rocked his hips into mine. Holy hell. This could go too far too fast.

I had to remember why I was here. *Why?*

"Axel," I breathed.

That one word instantly killed the moment.

"What?" Rylan growled, pushing off me.

"Keira said she saw Axel in town," I said, still breathless.

He didn't answer, but then a lamp clicked on, gilding his beautiful face. Dammit, he was so freaking hot.

"Axel's dead," he said, raking his fingers through his hair.

I sat up and adjusted my top. "Yes, that's what she said, but now, she's not so sure."

"Why wouldn't she be sure?"

"Because the body they found was headless. It had his clothes and ring, so they assumed it was him."

Rylan cursed.

"I'm sorry. I just thought you should know."

Rylan exhaled and his eyes softened. "Thank you. Did Karina see him too?"

"No. But Keira looked like she'd seen a ghost."

I couldn't read the expression on Rylan's face. But at this moment, I wished I hadn't killed what we had going. Because for that moment, the weight of the world had been lifted off his shoulders.

"I really am sorry," I said, standing from the bed.

"Come here," he said, his eyes still glinting with gold. As I stepped closer, he wrapped his arms around me. "Why are you sorry?"

"Because I was the bearer of bad news and completely killed our moment."

His hand traveled down my back, resting on my butt. "Oh, we'll have more mind-blowing moments. I'm sure of it."

"Even more mind-blowing than that last kiss?"

"Cupcake, you have no idea," he purred against my ear, sending a chill down my spine.

"Good. Then I have one more message." I grimaced, and he dropped his head and sighed.

"What is it?"

"Family meeting in—" I glanced at my watch—"forty-five minutes."

"I'll be there."

"I'm glad." I wrapped my arms around his bare waist and stole one more breathless kiss before slinking away. I knew if we were alone for any length of time, things would go from hot to inferno in no time.

CHAPTER 11

RYLAN

The entire family gathered in the living room at Piers's house. Even Barney's twins, Weston and Drake, showed up. I hadn't seen them in a few weeks, but they seemed to be getting taller. They weren't very talkative, probably because they were more involved in social media than socially interacting with real people. And they were gamers. Fortnite was their newest obsession, and from what I'd heard, these boys were tearing it up online.

My shoulder was well on the mend. The incision had already sealed together, and the swelling had gone down. Benefits of being a wolf shifter.

The family gathered in the living room, and Eris sat next to me on the love seat, her body pressed against mine. I didn't know what it was about her that drove me crazy. Maybe the fact that she was getting closer to shifting. But everything about her appealed to me. And every day it seemed to get stronger. Her inner wolf was connected to mine, and I knew she felt it, too.

I ran a finger down her arm and watched goose bumps rise. It took everything inside of me not to throw her over my shoulder and drag her upstairs. That, and the fact that her entire family was sitting around me.

Piers immediately took control and discussed the entire situation. A situation I never wanted them involved in. But they never showed any ill feelings or that they were disappointed in me. In fact, they were more worried about me and Keira and Karina, and were anxious to make sure we were safe and protected.

At the end of the discussion, Piers offered Karina a part-time job as a cashier at the Blaekthorn Lumber & Supply shop, and she graciously accepted. Then Garrick and Vera offered them their spare guest bedroom. It was next to mine, but I didn't mind. I'd lived with them most of my life, and they were happy to have a space all their own. At least, until they could save up enough to get their own place.

After the meeting was over, I pulled Keira to the side and questioned her about Axel. I didn't know how or why he was still alive and walking around Havenwood Falls, but right now, he was considered a threat. Axel was supposed to be alpha. He was supposed to be protecting his pack. If he was alive, well . . . he was better off dead.

After the meeting, the men made sure the area was secure, while the women started dinner. Steaks and ribs were grilling while side dishes were being prepared.

Barney even brought over his guitar and sang some songs around a bonfire. It felt like forever since we'd let go and had fun.

I watched Eris grab a drink from the cooler and make her way around the fire, the flames gilding the beautiful contours of her face. Then, she slowly stalked her way over to me, her golden eyes never leaving mine. If looks could kill, I'd be a dead man.

"Is this seat taken, sir?" she asked. But there was no seat next to me.

"You mean, this seat?" I asked patting my lap. She shrugged, waiting for my reply. "Well, miss . . . this seat is reserved for a special girl."

She smiled and leaned down, her hand on my forearm, her face inches from mine. "And who is this special girl?"

I shrugged. "You might know her. She's amazing. Gorgeous. Smart. Sexy. Witty."

"Hmm," she hummed. "I'm not sure."

Damn her. Those sultry eyes were glimmering in the firelight, drawing me in, deeper and deeper. If her family wasn't watching, I'd grab her and take her back to my room.

Instead, I took her arms and pulled her onto my lap. She wrapped her arm around my shoulder, and I hugged her waist.

The family didn't seem to mind. In fact, they all carried on as if we'd been a couple for a while. Even Piers glanced our way, with no looks of intent to murder me.

I guess I was fitting in. I just had to make sure I followed the rules to keep the peace. And Piers made sure I understood that his daughter was off limits until she was eighteen.

With Eris on me, the tension melted and I found myself laughing. For those few hours, we were ourselves. Enjoying each other's company, good food, and music.

With the strength of this pack—true strength and a real family bond—we didn't have to worry about Lars. He'd be torn to shreds if he came anywhere near this fiercely protective family.

My new family. The Blaekthorn Shadow Pack.

CHAPTER 12

ERIS

*H*e was there. The black devil, standing in the shadows. His red eyes pierced the darkness, watching, stalking. I looked around for Rylan, but there was no one else but . . . me.

"Who are you?" I asked, glaring into those demon eyes.

"I see why he chose you," he replied, pacing in the shadows.

"What are you talking about?" I shouted. "Come out here and face me, you coward!"

But he remained deep in those dark shadows.

"The pup thinks he can stand against me? He took my eye, so I'm going to take something even more precious from him. Something he cares deeply about. Something he . . . loves."

Love?

"Such a shame. You're a beautiful girl."

I gasped when he finally stepped out of the shadows. His face was horribly scarred; his right eye nothing but a deep, black hole.

"Stay the hell away from me," I warned as he stalked closer.

My mind was blank. I couldn't remember a spell. Any spell. And the wolf inside me was still slumbering. Dammit. Get up. Get up, you stupid wolf.

"Don't worry, cupcake. I'll make sure it's quick and painless."

"You bastard!"

I turned to run, but he bounded after me, knocking me to the ground. My face and hands raked against the pavement, the wounds burning as he pressed down on my back.

Where the hell was I? There was no landmark around me. Just a dark road and endless trees.

I couldn't breathe. Then I felt sharp claws raking, tearing through fabric and flesh.

"Help!" I screamed. "Help me!"

But no one could hear me. And no one would save me.

I WOKE, gasping for air, still feeling the prickling stings across my back.

I clicked on my light and was in my room, in bed. Sweat clung to me, soaking through my pajamas and making strands of hair stick to my face.

Safe. I was safe.

The phone rang downstairs, sending another shot of adrenaline through my veins. My heart hammered harder and faster as I glanced at the time. Who the hell would be calling at three in the morning?

I opened my bedroom door and clicked on the hall light just as the phone stopped. I exhaled and turned back into my room. But it rang again.

Maybe it was a family member. Or Rylan.

Without another thought, I ran down the stairs as my dad exited his room. He stood at the top, watching me closely, his eyes heavy with sleep.

I picked up the receiver, trying to steady my trembling limbs. "Hello?"

"Eris? Oh, thank the goddess," a familiar voice panted.

"Grandma?"

I looked up to my dad, who was trying to blink himself awake.

"Yes, darling. It's me. I'm sorry for calling so late."

"Is everything okay?"

"Yes. Yes, I'm fine," she said, trying to catch her breath. "I just had a terrible nightmare. It was about a demon wolf and . . . he was after you."

Goose bumps rose all over my skin. "Grandma, I just had the same nightmare."

"Oh, my darling Eris," she sighed, "what have you gotten yourself into?"

I swallowed a huge lump in my throat. "I don't know."

"Do you still have the Book of Shadows?"

"Yes, of course."

"I want you to look for a spell, and I want you to memorize it."

"Okay, which one?"

"It's called the Transportation Spell. It can teleport you from one location to another. But you must get it right or you could end up lost in the in-between."

"The in-between? Grandma, I don't know if I can—"

"Eris, listen to me. You are a Witheridge witch and a Blaekthorn wolf. Strength and power are coursing through your veins. Don't ever doubt that power, or yourself. Memorize the transportation spell, and if you should ever need to use it, think of someplace nearby. Someplace safe. Don't travel too far, because the farther you go, the easier it is to get lost."

"Are there any other spells that can kill him?"

"We never use a spell to kill. Those are dark and very complicated, and they require you to give something of yourself. The transportation spell is the easiest to learn, and it can give you a chance to save yourself."

I sighed, overwhelmed. "Can I ask you a question?"

"Of course, darling. What is it?"

"In your dream . . . did I die?" I saw my dad start down the stairs out of the corner of my eye.

She paused, and I knew the answer. I died in her dream.

"It won't happen to you, Eris. Your father and your family will protect you. Tomorrow morning, I'll make my way to you. So stay home. Stay with them."

"Okay," I said, my body trembling. But knowing she would be coming made me feel a little better. "I'll see you soon."

"Oh, and Eris . . . could you please send me directions to where you are? I can't recall how to get there."

"Sure, Grandma."

"Stay close to your family, Eris."

"I will." I hung up the phone and looked at my dad. Overwhelmed with emotion, I broke down and ran into his arms.

"What's the matter, sweetheart?" he asked, stroking my hair.

"I had another dream, and Grandma dreamed the same thing."

"What was it about?"

There was no easy way to tell him. "Lars killed me."

My dad stepped back, and the look in his eyes was one I'd never witnessed before. It was the look of horrible torment. A fear and sadness and rage all wrapped up together, ready to explode. He closed his eyes and steadied himself before gripping my shoulders firmly.

"Listen to me, Eris. You will not die, because I won't allow it. I am your father and your protector, and that bastard will die before he lays a hand on you. I lost your mother, and I swore to her that I would keep you safe. I will not break that promise. Do you hear me?"

I nodded and hugged him, and his large protective arms wrapped around me. I knew he would keep his promise. If he was able to.

Back in my room, I took out my great-grandmother's Book of Shadows and found the Transportation Spell. I repeated it, over and over, until saying the words became second nature. But it took much more than reciting words. It took belief and power to cast a spell.

I slid off the bed and stood in the center of my room. With authority and power, I spoke the words of the spell, three times. As I said the last word, I blinked, and the next moment, I was standing in my bathroom.

It worked! Holy hell, it worked!

I squealed to myself, having added one more spell to my arsenal.

I quickly used the bathroom, then repeated the spell and appeared back in my bedroom.

Oh man. I couldn't wait to use this one on Camden and scare the crap out of him.

~

THE NEXT MORNING, my dad kept me on a tight leash. I wasn't allowed to leave the house, and there was always someone with me. I begged him not to tell Rylan about what happened, but he said he had to, so he could help protect me. I guess it meant he trusted him, which was a good thing. And it wasn't only him. The entire family knew and had become guards.

But I was more worried about Rylan. The entire reason he left Havenwood Falls in the first place was to keep Lars away from me.

Aunt Vera walked in the door with a Tupperware of fresh baked chocolate chip cookies.

"I know you love these. Eat as many as you like. I won't watch."

"Thanks." I laughed, biting into a hot cookie. It was soft, and the chocolate melted in my mouth. "Where's Rylan?"

"I think he went into town," she said. "He said he'd be right back, then hopped on his bike and took off."

I stopped chewing. My chest felt like a hole had been punched through it. "How long ago did he leave?"

She cringed. "A couple of hours?"

I couldn't breathe. "We have to go find him. What if he left? What if he went after Lars?"

I ran upstairs and threw on some jeans and a jacket.

"Eris, you can't leave. It's too dangerous out there," Aunt Vera begged, chasing after me with her high heels on.

"I have to go," I demanded. "He was there for me when I needed him."

I was about to head out the door when I heard the rumbling of a motorcycle. I flung the door open as Rylan pulled into our driveway and shut off his bike. "Hey, cupcake, where are you headed to?"

I didn't know whether to kiss him or smack him for putting me through that stress.

"I didn't know where you were," I said, steadying my breath.

He slid off his bike with a wicked smile. "So, you were going to leave the house and look for me?"

I crossed my arms over my chest. "What if I was?"

"Then you'd be disobeying your father's order to stay home."

I shrugged. "Where did you go?"

He opened the saddlebag on his bike, pulled out a bag, and lifted it up.

"What's that?"

"Some things to kill time while you're on lockdown." He jogged up the stairs and stood in front of me. "You were going to break the rules for me?"

"You would have, for me."

"Damn right I would," he said, leaning over and kissing my lips before heading into the house.

I followed after him. "Wait, what's in the bag?"

He handed it to me, and I opened it up. "Cards and . . . board games? You play board games?" I wasn't sure if a wandering wolf shifter had time to learn or play games.

"Of course I play board games. Remember, I was here months before you."

I lifted a box out of the bag. "Uno and Boggle?"

"I'll have you know, I am the Boggle king."

"Oh, okay," I said, bowing. "Well, it's time to relinquish your throne, sire, because the queen is here."

"On lockdown, I might add," he noted with that wicked grin.

I sighed. "Yeah, whatever."

CHAPTER 13

RYLAN

*W*hen Piers told me about Eris and her grandmother's nightmare, I couldn't help but feel like shit and responsible for everything happening. Had I not come into her life, she wouldn't be in danger.

I'd thought about running again and hunting Lars myself, but decided to take another approach. One Eris would approve of. These were the cards life had dealt me, and now I had to figure out a way to play them the right way.

She made some snacks while I set up the games in the living room. We had fun, the two of us, laughing and teasing and bickering. She kicked my ass in Boggle, which sucked.

Our last card game, I was so way ahead, but she ended up throwing down a winning card, and I swear a few of mine disappeared.

"How the hell did that happen?" I huffed, scratching my head.

Eris threw her hands in the air and squealed, "Five seconds, baby!"

"What the hell is five seconds?"

She winked. "That's for me to know, and you to find out."

"You're cheating," I said, grabbing her by the waist and dragging her to the ground, tickling her.

Then, all of a sudden, she was gone.

"What the—"

"Want a drink?" she said from the kitchen, holding a can of soda, smiling widely.

"You used magic? That's how you won?" I hopped to my feet. "That's low, Eris Blaekthorn."

In a split second, she was standing inches in front of me, making my insides jump.

"Shit. You can't do that to me."

She threw her head back with a boisterous laugh, then wrapped her arms around my waist. "I admit it. I used magic to win." She looked up at me with her beautiful golden eyes and blinked. "Forgive me?"

At that moment I looked at her and knew—I could live the rest of my life with her.

Her hands caressed the back of my neck, pulling me down into a kiss. Her soft lips pressed against mine, her tongue slipping across them, begging for entrance. I obliged.

She was putty in my arms, both of us acutely aware of every place our bodies touched. Waves of heat surged inside me. God, I wanted this girl. As I kissed her again, a pleasurable moan ripped from her throat, and I answered with a soft growl, feral and desperate. My tongue delved between her lips, raking against her teeth, claiming every inch of her mouth.

I pulled away and murmured against her neck, "Forgiven."

She grabbed my ass and squeezed. "Holy hell, Rylan Gilles. You're going to get us into trouble." She ran a finger down my chest, almost too low, while biting her bottom lip. Then she slowly stepped back, pivoted, and swayed toward the TV, turning it on.

This girl would be the end of me.

Vera left to run some errands since I was there, and the rest of them had to work at the warehouse.

"What do you want to do now?" she asked, plopping down on the couch next to me.

"Tell me about your dream." I wanted to know details so I knew what we would be up against.

She lay her head down on my lap and looked up at me. "What did my dad tell you?"

A flicker of rage roiled in my gut. "That Lars killed you."

Her expression saddened, as if she were thinking back to her nightmare. "Yeah, that's pretty much what happened."

"Was it another premonition?"

She nodded. "My grandma called me right after I woke up, at three in the morning, telling me she had the exact same dream."

"Where were you . . . in the dream?"

"I don't know. I was standing on a road, but everything around me was dark. There was no landmark to tell me if I was in or outside of Havenwood Falls."

"And he was there?"

She nodded then turned her head away. "He talked to me. He said that because you took his eye, he was going to take something from you. Something precious. Something you . . . love." Her eyes met mine again. "He called me cupcake."

My body stiffened. "What?"

That bastard. How close was he for him to know my pet name for her? The thought woke my inner beast. I could feel him clawing at my skin, my sight turning red.

"Hey," Eris said, sitting up. She wrapped her arms around my neck and whispered into my ear, "It's okay. You're here with me. He can't touch me if you're here." Her fingers gently stroked down my back, calming the beast inside. I breathed in her scent, instantly feeling the rage melt away. No one else had been able to tame the beast inside. Not like her.

Lars would never touch her. I promised myself that. And I had to find a way to end it once and for all. I had to find him and kill him, even if I never got answers.

This time, it wouldn't be for me or for revenge.

This time . . . it would be for her.

CHAPTER 14

ERIS

*T*he entire reason why I didn't want to tell Rylan about the dream was because I knew he'd react and would probably feel like he had to do something to save me. I felt his wolf. I felt its rage, and knew it was seconds from ripping through his flesh.

I had to calm him, and used my inner wolf to speak to his. I put on a movie to try to distract his thoughts, and halfway through, he fell fast asleep. We were lying on the couch, my back pressed against his front, his arms wrapped around me. His warmth seeped through me like a blanket, so I snuggled closer to him.

I listened to the sound of his breath and the steady beating of his heart. A heart that had been through so much hurt and pain. A heart that had been broken and battered, but managed to survive.

I couldn't describe the emotions I had inside. It was a deep admiration, a wanting and yearning to be close to him, to get to know everything I could about him. He was so much more than what he projected himself to be on the outside, and he'd become a master at hiding his feelings.

But I knew I was chipping away at that massive wall he'd built around himself and his heart, and was slowly starting to get a glimpse of the true Rylan. A guy who would leave everything good he had behind, and risk death, to save me and my family.

The phone rang, and when Rylan stirred I carefully slipped from his warm embrace and ran to the phone.

"Hello?"

"Hi, this is Dr. Underwood from the Havenwood Falls Medical Center."

"Hi, doctor."

"I am trying to get in touch with Rylan Gilles. I called Garrick's home, but they said he was probably here."

"Oh, he is. Hold on, I'll get him."

I set the phone down and peeked over the couch. "Rylan," I whispered. "Dr. Underwood is on the phone."

He opened his eyes, sat up, then ambled to the phone.

"Hey, Dr. Underwood. This is Rylan." He turned to look at me. "Okay . . . yes." His voice became low, and his eyes distant. "Are you sure?" His face went rigid. "Thank you, doctor. I appreciate it . . . Bye."

Rylan hung up the phone and ran his fingers through his hair.

"What is it?" I stepped toward him, my stomach knotting, hoping it wasn't the news I suspected.

"He is definitely related to me." He sat down on the stairs, and buried his face in his hands.

"How closely?"

"I don't know. But no one ever mentioned another relative. Not my grandparents, not my parents, and not my pack. And even if he is related . . . why? Why would he kill my father in cold blood?"

I shook my head. "Something must have happened for him to snap."

"I don't think I'll ever find out. Everyone who would know the answer—except Lars—is dead."

"Maybe not everyone."

Rylan glanced up at me.

"If Keira saw Axel, then he must know. You said he was part of the pack and was your father's best friend."

"He could be anywhere."

"If he came to town and stayed for any given length of time, he would have to register. All supernaturals do. And I think that Addie Beaumont would know."

I picked up the phone and dialed the number on the card Addie had given me when she'd given me my tattoo.

When she answered, I quickly told her our situation, and then handed Rylan the phone for him to describe what Axel looked like. Addie told him that he had come into town about two weeks ago, and she gave him his tattoo. He was quiet, but she remembered him telling her he was going to explore Havenwood Falls and was there to camp, and wasn't sure how long he was going to stay.

A car was heading down the pavement, and when I looked outside, I saw my grandma's hatchback heading toward us. "My grandma's here."

Rylan smiled and nodded, and I ran outside to greet her.

She hadn't come as the Grinch, the old woman she glamoured herself to look like while in New Mexico. No, she was the beautiful woman, tall and slender, with long, golden hair braided down her back. She was wearing a white pantsuit with a tan trench coat over it.

She was even more beautiful than I'd remembered, and didn't look like she could be my grandmother. Suddenly, calling her Grandma didn't seem to fit.

"Eris, my darling," she said, spreading her arms wide for a hug. I wrapped my arms around her and was so glad she was here—another layer of protection.

"Grandma, it's so good to see you."

"Well. Let's get back inside. It's freezing out here."

"It's nice to see you, Gertie," Rylan said.

"It's nice to see you as well, Rylan." My grandma turned to me with a smile and wink, making me blush.

"So, tell me what's going on. Why my granddaughter is in danger."

We updated her about the entire situation with Lars.

"Grandma, could you use a location spell on him? Like the one you used to find me here?"

"Yes, but I would need something that belongs to him."

I glanced over at Rylan. "What about his tooth?" He shrugged, then we turned to Gertie. "The clinic has Lars's tooth. They extracted it from Rylan's shoulder and used it to do the DNA test."

"That would definitely work. If we can get it, I can find his location."

Rylan looked up the number and dialed the clinic. "Dr. Underwood said they have the tooth, but he'll only be at the clinic for another twenty minutes. I'm going to run and get it."

I walked up to him. "Please be safe."

"You be safe," he said, kissing my cheek.

"Don't worry. She will be," Gertie said.

Rylan nodded, and headed out the door. He jumped into the company truck and headed down the gravel path.

CHAPTER 15

RYLAN

I made it to the clinic with a few minutes to spare, and Dr. Underwood gave me the tooth. Slipping it into my jacket pocket, I headed back toward the truck. A familiar scent caught my nose. I whipped around to see a man in a dark trench coat quickly dart behind the side of the building, so I gave chase.

As soon as the man saw me, he sprinted toward the nearby woods. *Damn it.* "Axel!" I hollered, but he quickened his pace. "Axel!"

He was fast, but I was faster. Right before he hit the tree line, I dove forward and tackled him to the ground. A growl ripped from his throat, and his eyes turned golden. He was going to shift.

"Axel, stop," I yelled, sitting on his back, holding his arms behind him, pressing his face into the ground.

"Get off of me!" he bellowed, trying to buck me off. But he was never as strong as I was, and I held him down.

"Why? Why are you here?" I demanded.

"To watch over them."

"Who?"

"Karina and Keira. They're the last of our pack."

"Why did you fake your death?"

"Because Lars was going to kill me. He picked off the weak,

71

taunting me. He said I'd be last and he'd make it slow. So I had to fake my death, to survive."

"You're a coward!" I spat, twisting his wrists upward. He wailed in pain. "You're the pack's alpha. They depended on you and you left them vulnerable."

"I know," he said, and stopped fighting me. "But so did you." Those words were a knife to my chest. I let him go, and he moaned, rolling over and rubbing his sore wrists. "You were next in line to be alpha, Rylan. I was just a replacement."

I got up and paced. "My mother asked me to leave with her. She thought if we left, it would save the pack."

Axel looked up at me. His face was gaunt, his eyes sunken in, like he hadn't slept in weeks. "Lars won't stop until every member of the pack is dead."

"Why? Why is he doing this?"

Axel sighed and stood to his feet, scanning the area around him.

"It started way back, when your grandmother was pregnant with your father. A single girl within the pack had also become pregnant, but she told everyone she'd met a man at a nearby tavern, and they shared drinks and spent the night together. When she woke the next morning, he was gone, and left her with child.

"No one suspected anything, because she was young and beautiful and liked to party."

"How was she a member of the pack?" I was curious, because our pack was carefully chosen. A single party girl didn't seem like a choice my grandfather would make.

Axel shrugged. "Her brother was your grandfather's best friend. They grew up together. And when he asked to join the pack, your grandfather welcomed them."

I nodded, and he went on.

"Your grandmother and the girl became friends, having their pregnancies so close. They were always together, and everyone in the pack anticipated their births. They even made bets on who would go into labor first.

"It was a night when the moon was full, when the girl gave birth. Your grandmother was there to help deliver her baby boy, whom she named Lars. A few days later, your grandmother gave birth to your father—Barin.

"What no one knew, except Lars's mom, was that Barin and Lars were half-brothers. Only days apart, they grew up as best friends. But it was Lars who showed signs of being an alpha, and during their teen years, he had grown bigger and stronger than Barin.

"When they both shifted for the first time, Lars was a foot taller than Barin, but he also started to look an awful lot like your grandfather. When your grandmother brought it up to your grandfather, he denied it. But she couldn't deny the resemblance this boy had to her husband. Your grandmother felt it in her bones, that Lars was his son, so she confronted him once more, and he finally told her the truth.

"Filled with a righteous fury, your grandmother shifted and nearly tore off your grandfather's head. But what hurt her more than the lies and the adultery was that her son's future as alpha of the pack was in jeopardy. Lars was her husband's firstborn, and would be the rightful alpha.

"When Lars found out who his true father was, he coveted the position of alpha. He wanted nothing more than to rule the pack, and the pack had already grown to love him.

"Lars had even found love. A girl who was fatherless and had lost her mother to disease. She was a wanderer, and had found the pack. Lars fell fast in love with her, and in his heart, had already wanted her to be his mate. Yes, she loved Lars, but as a friend and nothing more. He'd twisted their friendship in his mind, and didn't know that Barin also had fallen for the girl.

"Seething with fury and jealousy, your grandmother gave your grandfather an ultimatum. She threatened to leave him and take Barin with her, unless he banished Lars and his mother from the pack forever. The members of the pack would also be given one rule: to never speak of or mention Lars or his mother again.

"Your grandmother wanted to make sure that her son, Barin,

would be alpha. As he rightfully should have been, and not some bastard child.

"Your grandfather had no choice but to agree. He banished Lars and his mother and warned them never to return. When Lars found out the reason for their banishment, he went mad and tore up the camp. What made it much worse was that the woman he'd thought to spend the rest of his life with had chosen Barin to be her mate."

I exhaled loudly. This story was messing with me. My freaking emotions were everywhere. Lars was my uncle, and I couldn't help but feel some kind of pity for him. It wasn't his fault he was born a bastard child and then punished for it. And to think his half-brother stole the woman he loved . . . I could see how that could piss him off. But not enough to murder him and the entire pack.

Axel's eyes shifted around us, like he was looking for danger. But I sensed nothing. Maybe he was so used to being hunted that he couldn't help it.

"Is there more?" I asked.

He nodded. "When your grandfather died and your father became alpha, Lars came back one night and confronted him. Barin tried to be rational at first, but when Lars asked your mother to leave with him, your father snapped and charged after him. He punched Lars in the face, and when Lars threw him off, the pack surrounded him, protecting your father.

"Then you went and stood by your mother and held her hand. And then your mother stepped to Barin's side and took his hand, and Lars finally saw the family you'd become—a family he'd dreamed of having with her.

"Something inside of him went very dark, and he swore, in front of everyone, that they would all die. Because of them, he was stripped of everything—his home, his family, his pack, his love. And now he was out there alone, trying to survive and stay alive.

"Your father, fiercely protective of his family and his pack, demanded he leave and never return, or he would suffer death. The pack stood with their alpha. The same pack that had once loved Lars had now turned their backs on him."

I seriously didn't know what to say. This entire situation was a freaking mess, starting with my grandfather. If anyone was to blame, it was him. He poked his rod into a place he shouldn't have, and because of it, multiple lives were ruined.

"I know you went after the pack in Montrose. It was brave of you, and your father would have been proud." Axel turned his back to me. "I will never forgive myself for what happened to them. I was responsible, and I'm sorry."

He left, and I didn't chase after him, because I needed to get back to Eris.

Axel looked like shit, and I knew it was a physical manifestation of what was going on inside of him. But thanks to him, I knew the truth.

And now, I needed to find Lars.

CHAPTER 16

ERIS

The entire time Rylan was gone, I worried. Yes, his injuries had almost completely healed, but he was in bad shape the other night. And seeing him covered in blood . . . I didn't ever want to see that again.

I set Gertie up in my room, so while she put her things away, I made us something to eat.

And then I heard a vehicle coming down the driveway. I ran to the window and peeked out, glad to see Rylan was back safely.

When he came to the door, I swung it open. A crooked grin rose on his full lips.

"Miss me already?"

"No," I lied. "Just wondering if you got the tooth."

"Liar," he chuckled, slipping a small envelope out of his pocket and handing it to me. When I tried to take it, he held on. "I have some mind-blowing news to tell you."

"That sounds serious," I said, as he let go.

"It is. I think your entire family needs to hear it."

I sighed. "The suspense is going to kill me."

"Where's Gertie?" he asked, his eyes scanning the bottom floor.

"Upstairs. She drove a long way, so I told her to rest."

"Good." He grabbed my waist and yanked me tightly against him. His right hand cupped my neck as he pulled me in for a kiss. He took me by surprise, but I savored it, sliding my hands under his shirt and over his muscular back.

He flinched under my touch.

"Damn, cupcake. Your hands are freaking cold."

"And your back is warm. So, thanks . . . for the breathtaking kiss and hand-warming service."

"Happy to oblige."

Unwillingly slipping from his embrace, I called the warehouse and told my dad that Rylan had some very important news. He said they were finishing an order, and would be home in half an hour.

xxx

The entire family, including Gertie, Keira, and Karina, had gathered in our living room as Rylan began his story.

He told them about going to the clinic and running into Axel. Keira became ghostly white when he mentioned Axel, but then the entire room was still and quiet as he shared the story about his grandfather, Lars, and his parents.

Even after he was done, everyone was still quiet. But my father stood up and patted Rylan on the shoulder.

"Thank you," he said. "At least now we have a better understanding of where this Lars fellow is coming from. But to tell a pack you'll kill them in revenge is one thing. To actually commit the crime and keep killing and killing . . . that tells me something is not right in his head. I do agree he's had a terrible past, one that could justify him being bitter and enraged, but he took it to an entirely new level. One I'm not sure he can come back from, nor does it seem like he cares to.

"We could attempt to talk to him, but at this point, I don't think he wants to talk. He is so far rooted in his rage and revenge that there may be no hope for him." He turned to Rylan. "I'm saddened to hear the horrors he faced being banished and finding out the truth, and the pain it must have caused. But we are all given choices in life. Paths that will make us better and bring us closer to our end goals. Sometimes, hatred and rage can blur those lines, but if you look close enough, they are still there.

"Lars chose to murder your father, your mother, and all those others in the pack. They were his family—and he still chose to kill them. Because of that, I don't think he can be reasoned with. Because of that, he's a huge threat to my family. Especially my daughter. If that man comes near her, so help me God, I will have no problem ripping out his heart and personally handing it to the devil."

"And I will do the same," Rylan said, proving his loyalty to me and the family.

My father gave him a nod.

"That guy has no clue what he's up against," Camden said, arms folded over his chest.

"A rude awakening," Uncle Barney said.

"Or an early grave," Uncle Garrick added.

Keira and Karina had looks of hope in their eyes.

"If you need us, we can help," Karina said.

My dad smiled at her. "I think you've done more than enough. You've kept yourself and your daughter alive and safe against that madman. Please, allow us to take it from here."

Karina's expression turned to one of relief. They'd been running for too long and were still recovering.

"Thank you," she said.

Aunt Vera walked over to her. "Why don't you come and help us hold down the fort and cook dinner? We'll let the guys handle this one. And they'll be hungry when they get back."

"We'd like that," Karina said with a broad smile, wrapping an arm around Keira, who readily agreed.

Rylan glanced over to me and winked, making my heart patter.

"All right," my dad said, clapping his hands together. "Gertie will be performing a location spell. I'm not sure how it works, but tonight, we will find Lars and end this, once and for all."

Gertie needed a quiet place to do her spell, so my dad, my uncles, Camden, and Rylan stayed while the others, including Keira and

Karina, went home. I could tell they were relieved to not be a part of it. They'd run for too long. Now was their time to relax and enjoy life.

Gertie laid a map of Colorado on the floor and placed Lars's tooth in the center. She lit a few candles and while everyone was quiet, she recited a spell while waving her white wand over the map.

The tooth began to roll, and then it stopped—directly on an area where Havenwood Falls would be, only Havenwood Falls wasn't on any normal map.

"What if we use a map of Havenwood Falls?" Camden suggested.

"Do you have one?" my dad asked.

"Yeah. I got one from the Backwoods shop."

Gertie nodded. "Yes, a map of the area would make it a lot easier to pinpoint him."

Camden ran upstairs and right back down with a visitors map. He laid it on top of the other one. Gertie tried the spell again, and this time the tooth rolled right to the edge of the map—maybe a mile from where our cabins were.

"Dad?" My heart was hammering, my stomach knotting.

"He can't hurt you, sweetheart." My dad wrapped his strong, protective arms around me, then addressed the others. "Get ready. Meet me outside in five minutes." Both of my uncles and Camden nodded and left. Then my dad turned to Gertie. "Would you be able to come with us? To pinpoint his location?"

"Of course," she said, gathering the map and the tooth.

"I'm coming," Rylan said.

My dad let go of me and placed his hand on Rylan's shoulder. "Just remember, son—he wants you dead."

"I know. But if there is even a spark of good left in him, I have to try."

My dad nodded. "If he makes any threatening move, I won't hesitate to do what I have to, to protect my family."

Rylan nodded. "I know."

"Dad, since Gertie is going with you, and all of you will be there, I think I should go, too."

"No. You'll stay here with your aunts. They are fierce and can protect you."

"I'll stay in the car. What if he slips through and all of you are out there? Gertie can put a glamour over the vehicle, so he won't even know we're there."

His eyes averted to Gertie. "Can you do that?"

"Of course I can," she said. "Glamours are a specialty of mine. Remember the Grinch?"

"Boy, do I," my dad sighed loudly. For a moment, we all laughed. "Is there a way to put a glamour over the entire vehicle for the entire ride? So he doesn't know we're coming?"

"I can." She didn't even have to think about it. I'd seen Gertie's magic and knew she was powerful.

My dad turned to me with seriousness in his eyes. "You can only come if you promise to stay in the vehicle with Gertie."

"Deal," I said. And that was that.

I gave Rylan a smile, but I knew he wasn't thrilled I was going. Especially after the dream I'd had. But I wasn't alone. Because of that premonition, I would be able to create a new outcome. I just hoped that no one would get hurt in the process.

CHAPTER 17

RYLAN

*T*he ride in the Expedition to find Lars didn't seem to faze the Blaekthorns. It was obvious they'd been in a lot of situations like this one. They were experienced. Probably even more experienced than Lars.

Inside, I felt the tension building. This was it. Live or die. Good or bad. My life, after tonight, would never be the same.

I couldn't help but wonder how broken that man was. Was he damaged beyond repair? I'd done some things I'd regretted in my past, but never like this. Sometimes, you need to kill to survive. But killing someone just because you are pissed at them is not a justifiable reason.

"He's right outside the border of the town limits," Gertie noted. She'd glamoured the car, so no one could see it.

I was sitting in the back seat next to Eris, with Gertie on her other side. Barney and Camden were in the seat in front of us, and Piers and Garrick were in the front. Piers sped toward the location Gertie had given him, his eyes already glowing yellow in the rearview mirror. He was ready for whatever was to come.

"He's close," Gertie finally said, and Piers slowed the vehicle.

I squeezed Eris's hand, and she gripped mine tightly, like she didn't want me to let go. I stared into those beautiful golden eyes and nodded, then she lay her head on my shoulder.

"Stay with me," she whispered into my ear.

"I'll be back," I promised, pressing a kiss to the top of her head.

"Stop," Gertie said. Piers put on the brakes.

"Rylan, promise me you won't risk your life."

"I promise you this: I'll do what needs to be done. Nothing more. Nothing less."

CHAPTER 18

ERIS

We stopped in the middle of a road, and it became hard to breathe. The sides of the road were shrouded in darkness, as were the trees beyond. It was the exact same place as in my dream.

But it was only a dream. This time, I wasn't alone.

"Where is he?" my dad asked.

Gertie swiped her wand over the map. "On the left. Just beyond the shadows. He heard the engine. He knows something is going on."

"Can you put a glamour over us?" Barney asked.

"Not all of you. Maybe one more."

"Then put it over me," my dad said.

"I'll go out and distract him," Rylan added. "That way you can get in a good position to take him out."

"Rylan," I breathed. "You can't."

"I have to," he said, taking both of my hands. "I have to try. Besides, your dad will be there."

"I will," my dad answered. "Just don't get too close to him."

Uncle Garrick patted my dad on the back. "Barney and I will be ready. As soon as anything goes down, we'll be there."

My dad nodded. He knew he could count on them. Then he

turned and nodded to Rylan. Rylan opened the door and stepped out, while Gertie put a spell over my dad. As soon as my dad opened the door and moved away from the vehicle, he disappeared.

My pulse started to race as Rylan stepped away from the vehicle, my eyes locked on the shadows. It was like watching a scary movie unfold in front of me, only this was real.

Then, just like I'd seen in my dream, one red eye appeared, glowing in the darkness.

Rylan walked into the dark road with his hands in the air. "Lars, I know you're out there," he said loudly.

A deep growl reverberated in the air. "You've come to die, pup?"

Rylan took another step forward. "You don't have to do this."

"Shut up!" he roared.

I could hear Lars. "How can I hear him when I'm not in his pack?" I said, mostly to myself.

Everyone in the car turned their attention to me, their eyes narrowed.

"You can hear the wolf?" Uncle Garrick asked, and I nodded.

"Your mother had the same gift," Gertie replied, laying a hand over mine. "She was able to hear wolves from different packs."

There was so much I needed to learn about my new gifts. So much I was learning about my mom.

"Step closer," Lars continued, "so I can take a good look at you before I rip your throat out."

"I know who you are, Uncle," Rylan said slowly and cautiously.

The huge black wolf stepped into the street. His face was marred, a black hole in the place of one eye. Hackles were raised on his back, and lips were curled over razor sharp fangs.

"Don't *ever* call me uncle," he growled. "We are *not* family."

My hands pressed to the glass, silently begging Rylan to back away. Then I watched the horror multiply right in front of my eyes, because six more wolves stepped out of the darkness and stood behind Lars.

And just like that, Rylan and my dad were outnumbered.

Fear overtook me, waking up my inner wolf, begging it to be set free.

Wake up, it screamed. *Wake up!*

"Eris," I heard my grandmother say. I turned to her, and the world around me was suddenly a bright red.

Something slammed into our vehicle. The force was so strong, Gertie whacked her head against the window and was knocked out. Her body slumped to the seat, and her wand dropped to the ground and rolled under the seat. The glamour instantly disappeared, and I heard another growl outside.

Twisting back, I watched Rylan shift, and something inside me stirred. Holy hell, that was hot.

Then my dad suddenly appeared, right behind Rylan. They were nearly the same size. Both huge alpha males.

Without hesitation, Camden and my uncles threw their doors open, immediately shifting before they touched the ground.

It was happening. But not the way it was in my dream. We were changing the outcome.

CHAPTER 19

RYLAN

I could smell them before they showed their faces. Members of my father's pack. Six of them. The bastards.

"Why?" I asked.

Lars snarled. "Because they know who their true alpha is. Their loyalty is to me, alone. They begged me to spare their lives so they could follow me. They wanted me to be their alpha and lead their pack. How could I refuse?"

I growled. "I thought you killed them."

"I did kill those who tried to stand against me. So, in a way, you could call what I did . . . self-defense. After the troublemakers were gone, it was easy for the others to follow me."

Lies. These men were cowards and only joined him to save their own asses.

"How could you kill your own family?"

He growled and snapped his teeth, spittle flying. "I told you. I have no family. Everyone who died deserved to die."

"And what about you? You murdered my father and mother for protecting their family."

"You know *nothing* about me!" Lars roared. He was circling me, and the others behind him were getting closer, braver. I knew then there was no reasoning with him. I tried, but he was too far gone. "You will die tonight, and everyone who came with you will die too."

A loud crash had me turn around to see the vehicle suddenly appear in the road. Then I saw Eris turn, her golden eyes wide with fear and frozen on me.

"What a delicious treat," Lars taunted. "She'll be mine before the end of the night."

Rage ignited inside, and I shifted, letting my inner beast break free.

This bastard was going to die.

I heard Piers growl behind me, and knew his brothers and Camden were right behind. I didn't care if they outnumbered us. These cowards, who would stand up against me and be party to Lars's plan to murder me and threaten my girl and new family, would die. They were no match for us.

Lars bounded forward like a rabid dog, foaming at the mouth, his one eye filled with so much hate and madness. I charged forward to meet him, dodging his sharp teeth aimed for my face. I caught his left leg in my jaws and snapped them shut. With my forward momentum, I pulled him away from Eris. A flick of my neck sent him tumbling down the road.

I turned back to see the others. The Blaekthorns stood strong against the six others. Those six growled and bared their teeth, but they didn't move to fight.

"Rylan!" I heard Eris scream. I turned back to see Lars bounding toward me. He leapt forward, but I couldn't dodge him fast enough.

CHAPTER 20

ERIS

*M*y heart beat so loudly I could hear it in my ears. Then Lars made his move.

Rylan moved like lightning, swift and smooth, avoiding Lars's first strike. Then he struck, latching onto Lars's leg and dragging him away from us. I wasn't breathing, watching the events unfold.

My dad, uncles, and brother stayed near the truck, protecting me and Gertie, ready to fight the six others who had joined Lars. But the wolves only stood in the road, their eyes on Rylan and Lars, and it appeared they had no intention of fighting.

When I turned back, Rylan's eyes were on them, so he didn't see Lars charging at him from behind.

"Rylan!" I screamed.

He turned as Lars was in the air, and there was no way he could avoid him.

I quickly recited a spell from the Book of Shadows, and the world around me froze.

Five seconds.

A few more spoken words transported me right next to Rylan. I shoved his huge wolf form to the side, and as soon as the world unfroze, we both fell to the road.

A hair-raising growl erupted from Lars as his teeth and claws met nothing but air. He turned, his one evil eye glaring at us, his teeth bared and dripping with saliva.

Rylan was on his feet in a split second, placing himself in front of me, protecting and shielding me from Lars.

Then I felt it. Felt the power of the wolf inside. It had finally awoken.

Lars stepped back, watching me with a sated glint in his eye.

I'd heard the first time you shifted was brutal. The raw intensity of the beast inside dropped me to my knees. I screamed in utter pain as my human body shifted. It felt as if I were dying. And the pain . . . the pain was utterly excruciating. I could barely breathe.

Every one of my bones cracked and snapped into a different form. The flesh—the human flesh—tore apart as the wolf broke free.

I heard my dad calling out to me, but his voice was muted, and I couldn't answer. The agony consumed me.

"I'm here, Eris. He won't hurt you," Rylan said, standing close by.

When Lars moved, Rylan took a step toward him, posturing. A low growl of warning ripped from his throat.

Then, as quickly as the pain of shifting came, it subsided.

I slowly stood to my feet—new feet. Four wolf feet.

Wobbly at first, I quickly felt my body and muscles and tendons strengthen. In my new wolf form, I stepped next to Rylan, and his golden eyes met mine, approving.

A deep, rumbling growl ripped from Lars.

Without warning, Rylan shot toward him. Head down, he slammed into his chest, then swiped a paw across Lars's snout, slicing flesh. Lars roared in pain, but took the blow and steadied himself. His wicked eye watched for the moment to strike. He paced from side to side, that red eye set on Rylan.

"Eris!" My dad bounded toward us, but the six finally attacked, stopping him in his tracks. My uncles and Camden jumped in, but I couldn't focus on them. I knew they'd take care of each other.

Lars charged forward, and as Rylan went to meet him, claws flew and teeth snapped. Rylan got caught in the face and leg, while Lars suffered another harrowing blow to his chest.

Lars struck again and again. His relentless rage fueled his fight. But Rylan fought back, strong and fast, matching the older wolf's strength. Blow after blow, through countless slashes and bites, Lars was starting to pant. He was tiring.

In a last-ditch effort, he let out a deafening growl. His face twisted, and his hind legs pushed forward, shoving Rylan backward. Rylan lost his footing and stumbled back, exposing his neck. Then I watched Lars's eye fix on its target.

As if in slow motion, I watched him pounce, his mouth wide, teeth bared, and his intent obvious. He was going for his throat. He was going for the kill.

All I could do was move. My new strong legs thrust me forward directly into his path, and Lars's teeth sunk deep into my back.

I wailed as pain shot through me, like knives tearing into my flesh.

In a split second, Rylan leapt over us, and in mid-air, sunk his teeth into the back of Lars's neck and yanked him back. Lars yelped and released his grip on me. I hit the ground with a thud. I couldn't move. I couldn't breathe. Warm liquid soaked my new golden fur.

"Eris, stay down," my dad commanded. I looked over to him, still engaged in battle with my uncles and brother. They were all still standing.

I turned to see Rylan land on his hind legs, the back of Lars's neck still clamped tight in his jaws. A raging fire burned in his eyes. I could feel his power pulsing around me—the power of an alpha.

Rylan flipped Lars over his head, slamming his body onto the ground, the air exiting his lungs. Rylan then clamped his jaws around Lars's throat.

"Rylan, stop!" A large man exited from the woods wearing a dark trench coat.

Lars was weakened, his breath slow, suffocating as Rylan squeezed.

"Rylan, don't do this," Axel coaxed, stepping in front of them. "Don't let his blood stain your hands." Axel took a step closer. "Let go."

Rylan's eyes finally met Axel's, his chest panting heavily, then slowly . . . slowly, his jaw dislodged from Lars's neck.

CHAPTER 21

RYLAN

*L*ars was winded, but the bastard was freaking determined. Catching me off guard, he shoved me backward, his jaw open, teeth bared, ready to bite. Before I could right myself, Eris came flying out of nowhere, throwing herself in front of me.

My heart stopped as I helplessly watched his sharp teeth—meant for my throat—sink into her back.

When Eris yelped in pain something inside of me snapped. An anger. An all-consuming rage was set ablaze. He'd touched her. He hurt her. And now he was going to pay.

I jumped over them and sunk my teeth into the base of Lars's neck and yanked back, forcing him to release. And when he did, I slammed his body to the ground. Before he could make a countermove, I sunk my jaws into his throat and clamped down. I wanted him to feel his impending death. To know it was near and fear it, like he'd done to all of his victims.

Then, beyond the pounding rage in my ears, I heard a voice.

"Rylan, stop!" But I didn't want to stop. He'd hurt Eris, and I swore he would never touch her again.

Lars gasped for breath, but I held on, clamping tighter, obstructing his airway.

"Rylan, don't do this," Axel begged, standing in front of me in his human form. "Don't let his blood stain your hands." Axel took another step closer. "Let go."

Bastard. He should have let me have my moment and finish him, once and for all.

But he was right. *Damn it.* If I killed Lars, I would be no better than him.

When Lars went limp, I finally let go and ran over to Eris.

She was lying on the ground, blood coating her beautiful golden fur.

She'd shifted for the first time, when danger had presented itself, and she proved her true strength. But also, as soon as she shifted, I felt an invisible bond, a thread, tighten between us.

She was mine. I'd known it from the start. And no one, including any freaking last blood relative, was going to take her away from me.

I walked up to her and nudged her nose with mine, then said, "I'm sorry." Even though I knew sorry wasn't good enough.

She lifted her head, her golden eyes filled with pain.

"For what?" she exhaled.

"He hurt you. I broke my promise."

She shook her head. "Maybe I wanted to be the hero, for once."

"Rylan!" Camden howled. I turned to see Lars standing back on his feet, foaming at the mouth. But before we could do anything, Axel shifted into his gray wolf form and attacked. He and Lars tumbled off the road and into the dark trees.

Sounds of gurgling and choking, then bones snapping, shattered the night. Then it went quiet.

Axel walked out into the street, blood dripping from his maw.

"It's over. Lars is dead. You're free," he sighed and closed his eyes. "We're all free."

Garrick and Barney ran over to the side of the road and confirmed it.

He was dead. It was over. It was finally over.

Back in our human forms, we made our way back to the vehicle, but Axel stood off to the side.

"Do you have someplace to go?" I asked.

He gave me a broad smile. "Anywhere I want to now, without worry." He pulled his coat around him tightly. "I think I might head north, to Canada. I have a sister there, and a nephew and niece I've never met. I'd like to visit them. And then I'll see where I go from there."

"That sounds nice, man."

Axel looked behind me.

"You've got a good thing going here. I don't blame you one bit for leaving the pack." He gave me a sad smile. "And don't worry about the ones who got away. They're happy to be free. They're probably far away, headed toward other states by now."

I laughed and couldn't help but feel sorry for him. I extended my hand. "Thank you, Axel. You came through tonight."

He nodded. "Thanks for taking care of Karina and Keira. Please tell them I'm so sorry."

"I will."

He turned to leave, but he paused and turned his attention back to me. "Your father and mother would be proud."

For the first time since my parents died, tears slid down my cheeks. "Thank you."

And then he left. I knew it was probably the last time I would see Axel.

Back in the car, Gertie was fine. She had a little bump on the head, but she said it was nothing a few aspirin couldn't take care of. Everyone else had minor injuries and scratches, but it was Eris I was most worried about.

I sat on the seat with her head in my lap, because Gertie put a sleeping spell on her so she wouldn't have to deal with the pain. Everyone in the car seemed in high spirits, especially while Camden was telling his battle story. But I felt numb, thinking back to the moments that brought us here. So much had happened in such a short amount of time that it felt like I was living in some twisted dream.

Then Camden said, "They had no chance with the Blaekthorn Shadow Pack and the Witheridge spells."

"Shadows and spells definitely won tonight," Piers agreed. "And it seems Eris is now a part of both worlds."

"She'll be unstoppable. A force to be reckoned with," Camden said, and everyone agreed.

I smiled at the girl sleeping in my lap. My girl. My cupcake. She was not only beautiful, but she was brave and selfless. In the span of the evening, she'd saved me—not only once, but twice. First, with her magic. And then in her wolf form. God, I'd never hear the end of it.

Eris was wild and untamed, but so was I. We were rule breakers, but only when it served the greater good. And because of it, our lives and the lives of others were saved.

EPILOGUE

ERIS

Things changed after the night Lars was killed. My dad contacted Sheriff Kasun and discussed the situation, and the police took care of the body. My injuries healed quickly, and so did everyone else's. But the excitement came from the fact that I'd finally shifted, and proved to myself that I was a real member of the Blaekthorn pack. It also gave my aunts another reason to throw a huge party and celebrate.

Gertie drove back to New Mexico, after staying a week to make sure I was okay, and promised that by the end of summer she'd come back to Havenwood Falls to live. She wanted to be closer to the family and help me master the spells in the Book of Shadows, strengthening my magical side—the Witheridge witch side. I was looking forward to it.

Karina and Keira made a decision to leave and head back to their home country of Brazil, where most of their family still lived. When my dad presented them with plane tickets, they both cried.

"We could never repay you for your kindness," Karina said.

My father laid a hand on her shoulder. "It's a gift, and we don't want or expect anything in return."

They were blown away at his generosity, and after a few weeks, they were gone.

Rylan also changed after that night. The enormous stress and burden he'd been carrying on his shoulders had been lifted, and it was visibly noticeable. He invited me to most of his Havenwood Falls High activities, even dances, and introduced me to other students who would be attending next year, when I would be entering as a senior.

Rylan and Camden continued to work for the family business. Rylan was saving up enough money to build a cottage on a private piece of the property they'd given him.

We spent a lot of time together that spring, and our relationship blossomed. Rylan graduated from high school. I couldn't have been prouder, watching him walk down the aisle—this cocky guy who had stormed into my life one day and never left.

Because I was still seventeen and he couldn't claim me yet, he gave me a promise ring. It was perfect—a turquoise stone with an infinity symbol twisted on the side of a simple silver band. It was a promise that one day, we'd seal that undeniable bond that had already connected us. Until then, we enjoyed each other's company.

Rylan and I both found ourselves in this magical little town called Havenwood Falls, and had everything we could have ever wanted right around us. Love, family, friends, and . . . each other.

There was really nothing more I could ever want, besides my mom. Although my glimmer had left me—that tiny ball of light that would come and visit me, bringing me peace and warmth during my darkest times as a child . . . the glimmer which I found out was my mom—I knew she was still with me. She'd always be with me. And knowing that made living life so much easier.

RYLAN

On Eris's eighteenth birthday, I claimed her. We sealed that invisible bond that had connected us, and it was beyond anything I could have ever imagined. Beyond what either of us could have imagined.

I just wished my parents had met her, because they would have loved her.

The Blaekthorn family had already accepted and supported our relationship. They'd taken me in and treated me like a member of the family.

But it was Eris who had given my life new meaning. She helped me see and understand that my past didn't define me. If anything, it made me stronger.

I welcomed the future and whatever it had in store for me . . . for us. But no matter what it brought—the highs and lows, the good times and bad—I knew, deep down in my heart, that we would get through it together. One day and one breath at a time.

I'd finally found my place in life and a reason to exist. Here, in this magical little town called Havenwood Falls, I'd found home.

WE HOPE you enjoyed this story in the Havenwood Falls High series of novellas featuring a variety of supernatural creatures. The series is a collaborative effort by multiple authors. Each book is generally a stand-alone, so you can read them in any order, although some authors will be writing sequels to their own stories. Please be aware when you choose your next read.

Other books in the Young Adult Havenwood Falls High series:

Written in the Stars by Kallie Ross
Reawakened by Morgan Wylie
The Fall by Kristen Yard
Somewhere Within by Amy Hale
Awaken the Soul by Michele G. Miller
Bound by Shadows by Cameo Renae
Inamorata by Randi Cooley Wilson
Fata Morgana by E.J. Fechenda

Forever Emeline by Katie M. John
Reclamation by AnnaLisa Grant
Avenoir by Daniele Lanzarotta
Avenge the Heart by Michele G. Miller
Curse the Night by R.K. Ryals
Blood & Iron by Amy Hale
Shadows & Spells by Cameo Renae
Falling Deep by J.L. Weil
Saving Infiniti by Rose Garcia (December 2018)

More books releasing on a monthly basis. Stay up to date at
www.HavenwoodFalls.com

Subscribe to our reader group and receive free stories and more!

ABOUT THE AUTHOR

Cameo Renae was born in San Francisco, raised in Maui, Hawaii, and now resides with her husband and kids in Alaska.

She's a daydreamer and a caffeine and peppermint addict who loves to laugh and loves to read to escape reality.

One of her greatest joys is creating fantasy worlds filled with adventure and romance and sharing it with others. It is the love of her family and amazing support of her fans that keep her going.

One day she hopes to find her own magic wardrobe and ride away on her magical unicorn. Until then . . . she'll keep writing!

ACKNOWLEDGMENTS

Thank you, Kristie Cook, for creating this amazing world, and allowing me to play a part in it. You helped give life to these characters, and then edited and polished their journey. I don't know how you do it all, but you are truly amazing.

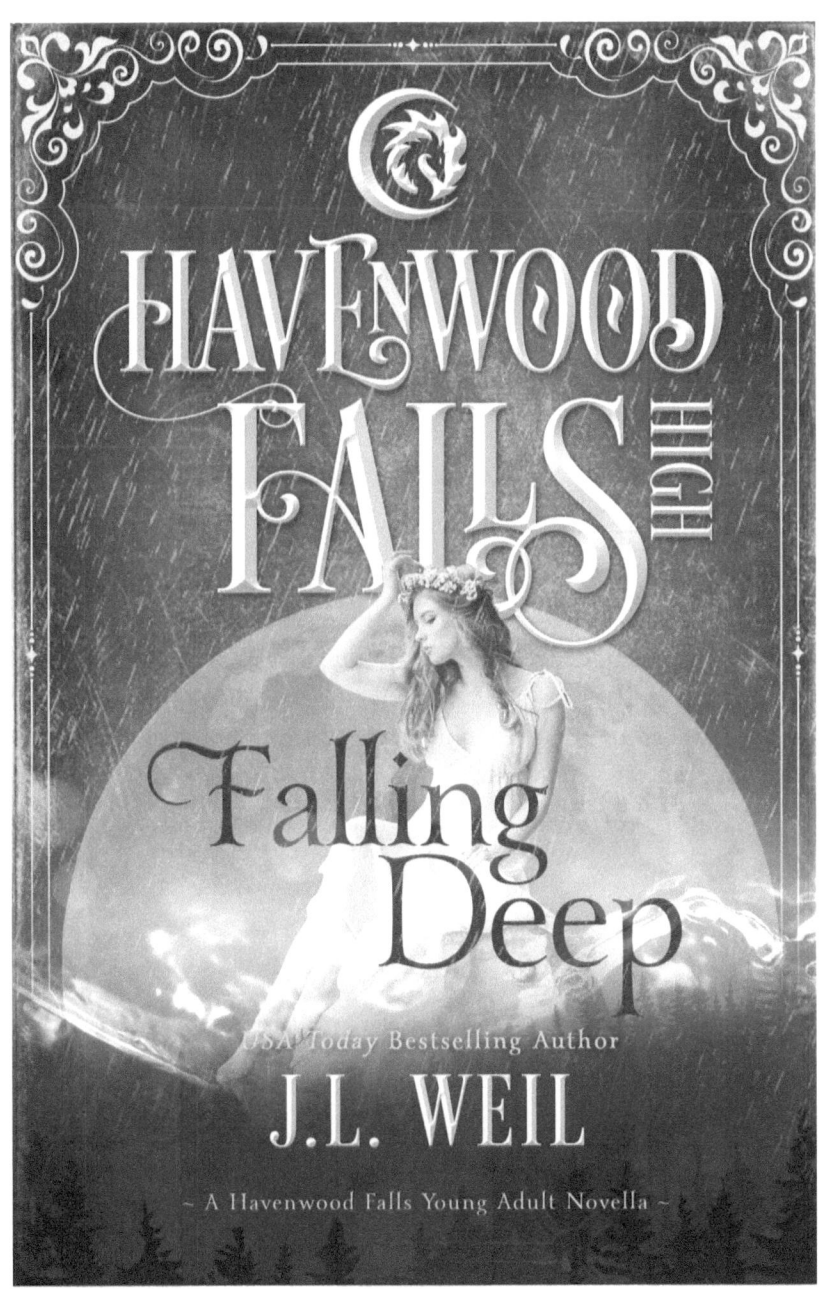

HAVENWOOD FALLS HIGH

Falling Deep

USA Today Bestselling Author

J.L. WEIL

~ A Havenwood Falls Young Adult Novella ~

Falling Deep (A Havenwood Falls High Novella) by J.L. Weil

More than any other aspect of high school, Mallory Dorian dislikes most the mean girls. Every school has them, and her new school, Havenwood Falls High, is no exception. Beautiful. Fearless. Popular. They are the kind of girls everyone envies but secretly hates. Why they decide to make Mallory's life a living hell, she can't figure out. Maybe she looked at one of them wrong. Maybe she took away all the attention, being the new girl. Or maybe it's because she is falling for one of their boyfriends—Torent Stark, the mysterious and troublesome guy whom she can't seem to get out of her head.

Take your pick.

It doesn't matter.

What does matter is she's a threat they're determined to obliterate. But Mallory has her own problems. From the moment she stepped foot into the quaint mountain town, something has awakened inside her. Something she's never felt before and can't define. The mystic and dark waters call to her, beckoning her to discover her true self. But to find out what she is, Mallory must first survive her initiation into Havenwood Falls High.

FALLING DEEP

I glanced in my rearview mirror, positive I was being punked. Nope. The boxes were still piled into the backseat of my aging Chevy Malibu. Forget trying to see out the back window. I had my whole life packed up in this hunk of junk.

Kind of sad.

Then again, my life was sad.

I was moving, leaving behind yet another house, another school, and another group of friends.

One year, I told myself. I only had one year left until I graduated, and then I could go wherever I wanted—live the life I chose—go to whatever college would have me. I only prayed this move didn't mess up my chances of getting a swimming scholarship.

I had worked too damn hard at being the best on my team. Correction—*had* been the best, but now that I was gone, the title went to Tiffany Hastings.

My fingers clenched on the wheel.

I'd miss a lot of things about living in Wisconsin, but Tiffany Hastings was definitely not one of them.

In a way, I was glad we were moving if it meant I would never again have to see Brady Cooper, the miserable bum Mom had been married to for the last two years. I wasn't going to miss his sorry face.

Mom had just signed the divorce papers from her third husband. Yep. Third. She wasn't lucky in love, or maybe it was because she only dated douchebags. And before the ink was even dry on the paper, Mom and I had our entire lives jammed into two cars, heading across the country to live in Havenwood Falls with my grandma, whom I called Gigi.

The town's stacked stone sign sat nestled between two flowering bushes, inviting and so cliché. I sank deeper into my seat, feeling anything but warm and fuzzy. "Welcome to Havenwood Falls" was written in black metal lettering.

I snorted. Welcome my left butt cheek. Finding this place had been a joke. I had nearly tossed the GPS out the window after the fourth time it tried to get me to turn around back the way I'd come.

Fortunately for us, Mom had been born here, yet still her sense of direction was crap. It was a freaking miracle we made it at all.

Let the suckage begin.

As I was reciting a list of things I already hated about Havenwood Falls, a streak of black darted out in front of my car, and reflexes kicked in as I slammed my foot on the brake. My poor car started to fishtail, and I knew this wasn't going to end well for either of us—the car or me.

I got one good glimpse of the creature before my car started to spin like a Ferris wheel on crack, and it didn't stop until the Malibu hit the ditch, snapping my head back against the seat.

Son of a—

God, that hurt.

I rubbed the back of my head, praying there was no blood. The last thing I needed was to pass out, and the sight of the metallic sticky stuff would do just that. I could handle lots of things—brussels sprouts, unnatural blondes, guys in thongs—but blood? Nope, no way.

My eyes flew out the window as I suddenly remembered the animal. I searched the road, looking for any sign of the critter. Had I hit it? Was it injured and lying hurt on the side of the street? Was I an animal killer?

Ensue panic attack.

I might be a lot of things, including the new girl, but I was definitely not a murderer.

But it was gone. Just vanished. My best guess? It had taken off into the woods after its brush with death.

Exhaling, I shifted the car into park and got out to check for damage. It wouldn't be the first mishap or dent Betsy had suffered. Betsy was what I called this piece of crap car. A few more dings would probably be an improvement, but really, I shouldn't complain. At least I had wheels to get me around. Not every seventeen-year-old could say the same.

As I glared down the road leading into Havenwood Falls, I realized Mom hadn't even stopped. Go figure. It would probably be a mile or more before she noticed I wasn't trailing behind her.

Fishing out my cell phone from the passenger seat, I sank back into the driver's seat and dialed her number. I left the door open, letting the crisp air of October rush over my face. She answered on the fifth ring.

"Hey, honey, you get lost?" Mom had a naturally husky voice that seemed to draw men to her like ants to a breadcrumb.

"Not exactly. I got run off the road."

"You what?" she shrieked in the shrill voice that always made me cringe. "By who? Another car?"

I rested my head on the back of the seat and closed my eyes for a moment. "Uh, no. It was an animal, I think. I'm going to need to call a tow truck."

"Are you okay at least?" she asked, suddenly getting around to worrying about my wellbeing. Mom wasn't what you would call responsible. She often forgot to turn off the coffee pot in the morning or pack my lunch when I was in first grade. I learned quickly how to take care of myself.

"I'm fine," I assured her. "Just another chapter to add to our adventure." Mom liked to think of each move—or *starting over,* as she so eloquently liked to say—as an adventure. I was tired of adventures and just wanted a place to call home.

"I'll turn around. Give me five minutes." Through the phone, I heard her flip on the blinker.

"Don't bother. I don't want to worry Gigi, and there's no need for us both to wait for someone to show up. I'll call you for directions as soon as my car is back on the road."

"Are you sure?"

"Positive. I'll just look up a towing company on my phone and give them a call. No big deal." So I kept telling myself. *I can handle this. It's time to start adulting.* Which I pretty much had been doing since I was ten. That was when husband number one had decided he'd had enough and split, walking out on us both.

I didn't know my real dad. Never had. One of the pitfalls of being a product of teen pregnancy. Eighteen-year-old prospective fathers don't always stick around.

We didn't need him.

"Okay, honey. Call me as soon as you're back on the road. The house is only ten minutes from where you are," she said. I could tell she was chewing on her lip, her nervous habit.

I assured her I would and hung up, immediately scouring the Internet on my phone for a local tow company. It took forever and a day for the search engine to load, and I blamed the soaring mountains. They were everywhere, and as breathtaking as the view was, my immediate concern was the crappy cell service.

"Come on," I encouraged under my breath, two seconds away from chucking my phone across the road. "Finally," I groaned as a single name and number popped up. *Havenwood Falls Garage & Tow Service.* Perfect. I clicked on the *Call Now* link and waited as the phone rang.

A gruff voice answered, and after I relayed my dire situation in way too much detail, he assured me help would be on the way in no more than twenty minutes. Crisis averted.

Now what to do to kill time? I tapped my fingers on the steering wheel before climbing out of the car. I left the keys in the cup holder and got my first real glimpse of the town I'd be living in for the next ten months. Come graduation, I was gone.

A river ran alongside the road near the base of the impressive mountains, bubbling faintly in the distance. The air was definitely crisp and cleaner as it moved in and out of my lungs. It seemed . . . peaceful, and I didn't know why that surprised me. Across the road was a quaint little neighborhood.

Pulling up the camera on my phone, I angled myself so the mountains were backdropped behind me and snapped a few selfies—okay, twenty, but I wanted to document the moment. My first catastrophe in my new home. Who wouldn't want that memory to laugh about someday?

I liked journals and scrapbooks. It was fun looking back on what was going on in my head or seeing the pictures of my friends. Wisconsin was far away now, including my old life. This marked my new journey aka stuck in hell, but regardless of the bad attitude, I would try for Gigi's sake to make the most of it. No moping around the house.

Fifteen minutes had passed when a truck pulled up, kicking dust in the air as I was snapping a picture of me in front of my poor car, angled so the trunk was sticking up in the air. I spun around and waited for the truck driver to get out. The name of the towing company was painted on the side of his cab. Tucking the loose strands of my honey-blond hair behind my ears, I smoothed the wrinkles from my hoodie. It had been a long drive, and I definitely wasn't looking my finest, but what did I care what some old grease monkey thought of me?

The door swung open and out stepped long legs covered in dark denim, but as the rest of him unfolded, my breath sort of stalled in my lungs. Broad shoulders lifted as he grabbed the side of the door, flashing a bit of defined abs. His jeans hung low on his hips, hugging a perfectly formed butt. My eyes traveled upward to his full, kissable lips, sharp cheeks, and stormy violet eyes fanned by sooty lashes. He looked down at me, the corner of his lip curving.

Holy crap. Nothing about the truck driver was greasy, saggy, smelly, or old.

His unusual and mesmerizing eyes captivated me, drawing me in until I felt as if I was floating in space.

Hot guy alert. Don't freak out. Don't freak out.

What did I do? I pocketed my phone and started rambling. "Thanks for coming. A thing jumped out in front of me, and I had to swerve off the road to avoid hitting it. Not exactly how I pictured my first day here, but maybe the universe is telling me something." *Someone stop me. Now! Before I give him my entire life story.*

"A thing?" he echoed in a deep, firm voice, lifting a condescending dark brow.

Internal wince. Hot guys made me nervous, and I couldn't be held accountable for the nonsense that came out of my mouth. "I'm not sure what it was—wolf or hellhound or bigfoot—take your pick. It was big and hairy."

His lips twitched. "If you say so."

A wave of embarrassment heated my cheeks.

He swept aside the half of his obsidian hair that was long, the other part shaved short. "Are the keys in the car?"

I nodded. "Cup holder."

He brushed past me to open the car door.

Damn. He smelled amazing, like insta-lust in a bottle.

I hated him. And wanted to have his babies at the same time.

"What are you doing in Havenwood Falls?" he asked as he dropped into the driver's seat, snatching up the keys. His eyes scanned the boxes in the backseat. "Vacation?"

"I wish," I groaned. "Divorce."

His questioning eyes found mine.

"Not me," I quickly clarified, feeling utterly mortified. "My mom. We're moving in with my grandma," I informed him, giving him more information than I normally would a total stranger.

"Sorry," he said, a glint of sympathy beaming in his gaze.

I hated being pitied, and my jaw tightened. "Nothing to be sorry for. Brady was a dick." Why was I telling him this?

"You should meet my brother. He takes being a dick to a new level."

I found my lips twitching, even though I didn't want to be amused by him. "And who would your brother be?" I fished. "Just so I can make sure to stay clear," I added so he wouldn't think I was hunting for information, which of course I was.

"I have two, but it's Brysen you have to watch out for. I'm Torent. Torent Stark. And you would be?" His smile reeked of trouble, and not the good kind.

"Mallory Dorian." I couldn't get over how perfectly symmetrical his face was, and I was damn sure his tongue was pierced.

"Who did you say your grandmother was? I probably know her. Havenwood Falls is that kind of town."

Swell. The corner of my lips curved. "I didn't say."

He shifted the car in neutral, and taking the keys with him, stepped out of the car. His full height, which I guessed to be just over six feet, forced me to tip my head back to look him in the eyes. Something about the violet color intrigued me, a glint in the irises that wasn't normal. He arched a brow as he waited for a name.

I had prolonged intentionally. "Layla Whitt."

"Seriously?"

My eyes narrowed. "What is that supposed to mean?"

"Nothing. I just didn't know she had a granddaughter."

He wasn't telling me something, and I wanted to press him. I didn't like secrets, and it had become clear that he was hiding something. "Yeah, well, this is my first time in Havenwood Falls. Actually, in Colorado."

"So you're a . . ." He left the unfinished question dangling as if he was second-guessing himself. Those unusual eyes bored into mine.

"I'm what?" I prompted, watching as he grabbed the hooky-thingamabob from the back of his truck.

He glanced over his shoulder while he secured the anchor under my car, and I caught the flash of a tattoo on his forearm. The movement had been too quick for me to get a clear view, but I was intrigued.

"A sophomore?" he posed.

That was so not what was on his mind. *What gives?* Torent Stark was hiding something, but why? What could he possibly know about me or my family? "No, I'm a senior."

Straightening up, he dusted off his hands on his jeans. "That's got to be rough, changing schools in the middle of a semester."

The sun was at his back, highlighting the sides of his cheekbones. Of all the people to meet first in Havenwood Falls, I had to encounter the most roguish of guys.

I shrugged. When hadn't my life been rough? "It's only seven months. I'll manage."

Something glittered in his eyes. "So you don't plan on sticking around after?"

Were all the people here this talkative? "Just long enough to graduate, and then I'm off to college."

Sauntering back to the truck, he wrenched open the door. "Havenwood Falls might surprise you. Who knows, you might find a reason to stick around." The lopsided smirk he aimed at me made my stomach cartwheel.

Was he implying *he* might be worth sticking around for? How presumptuous. I didn't even know him and wasn't positive I wanted to, regardless of how he made my insides react.

With that carnal grin still playing on his lips, Torent jumped into the truck to hit the button. In under a minute, my car was safely out of the ditch and back on the road. There might have been one or two scratches to commemorate my first day in Havenwood Falls, but I was more concerned about the mark Torent Stark had left on me.

"How much do I owe you?" I asked, tilting my head to the side as he slid out of the truck to lean against the side.

"It's on the house. Consider it a welcoming gift." A breeze blew through from the surrounding mountains, picking up pieces of his wind-tousled hair and sweeping them over one eye.

The urge to reach up and brush the loose strand of hair rose up inside me. I hadn't expected it.

"You really don't have to do that," I insisted, shoving my hands in my pockets before I did something stupid—like touched him.

"I know. But maybe you'll remember what a nice guy I was once you start school."

I gave him a funny look. "Are you saying you're not a nice guy?"

His gaze dropped and ran over my face. Something was there I couldn't quite grasp—a warning? "Definitely not. Welcome to Havenwood Falls, crash car. See you Monday." He dropped the keys into my hand.

Not if I can help it.

Slipping into the driver's seat, I put the keys into the ignition and turned. The car cranked over once before finally starting.

"Thanks for your help," I said, looking up at him with a straight face, the door still open.

He winked. "Anytime."

I didn't plan on making a habit of being rescued by Torent Stark. Something told me to stay far and clear from him. I sat in my car, frowning as Stark got into the truck. I knew guys like him. They were distractions, the kind that got you pregnant before graduation, and that was the very last thing I wanted.

To be my mom.

Purchase *Falling Deep wherever books are sold.*